# BACK TO WAR

## C. G. COOPER

**"BACK TO WAR"**

*Book 1 of the Corps Justice Series*

*By C. G. Cooper*

**>> GET A FREE COPY OF THE CORPS JUSTICE PREQUEL SHORT STORY, *GOD-SPEED*, JUST FOR SUBSCRIBING AT HTTP://CG-COOPER.COM <<**

This is a work of fiction. Characters, names, locations and events are all products of the author's imagination. Any similarities to actual events or real persons are completely coincidental.

This novel contains violence and profanity. Readers beware.

**REFORMATTED AND REMASTERED VERSION April 2018**

# DEDICATIONS

To my wife Katie for listening to all my crazy ideas. I love you.

In Memory of Lieutenant General Charles G. Cooper, USMC (Ret)

# PART ONE

# SECOND AVENUE, DOWNTOWN NASHVILLE, TENNESSEE

The gang members stayed hidden as they watched the young couple from the third story window of the parking garage a block away. The couple was blissfully unaware of the five observers. Why should they worry? They were in the middle of the busy downtown nightlife. Police were present as usual and the crowd flowed smoothly along the packed sidewalks.

The tallest of the gang was a thirty-something Black man named Dante. He had a short Mohawk cut and a pencil-thin goatee looked down at his latest recruit.

"You ready to do this thing?"

The young recruit looked no more than fifteen. His hazel green eyes starkly contrasted with his three-inch afro. He wore an oversized t-shirt with the New Orleans Saints logo plastered from front to back. His huge jeans were sagging and obviously way too big for his skinny frame. He looked like the prototype wannabe gangster. They called him Shorty.

"Yeah. I'm ready."

He was visibly nervous but vibrating with excitement. His drug-induced adrenaline kick was in full effect and he was ready to go. This would be his final step prior to being inducted into the small yet growing gang whose roots began in the hoods of New Orleans but were transplanted during Hurricane Katrina to the confines of Nashville.

The young couple they continued to track was chosen for one simple reason: they were white.

Most other gangs chose a less public criminal act for their young recruits. N.O.N. (New Orleans Nashville) had a special reason for choosing the outwardly normal pair. Although typically a subtle crew, their leader, Dante West, believed that the root of all the suffering he and his extended family had endured during the aftermath of Katrina was the fault of the white majority. Sure, there had been decent white folks who had helped with food and transportation, but his resentment was bred through the constant bombardment of the race-filled preaching of fellow gang leaders. *Shit, hadn't that badass rapper even said that the President hated black people?*

He believed his own gang now thrived because of two things: profitability and hate. Yes, Dante thought, that anger and emotion would help him grow N.O.N. to the size of some of the local Hispanic gangs. Also, Dante's cunning and expertise would further his expansion of N.O.N. The initiation ritual was the one deviation from his otherwise underground organization.

Dante looked down at his group of four brothers. "Now remember what I told you, Shorty takes the first hits. We only jump in if he starts getting his ass kicked."

The other members laughed out loud as Shorty spit out a nervous chuckle. "I ain't gonna get my ass whooped, Dante. That white boy is gonna get his ass whooped."

"I know, I know. You just do this thing right and tonight we'll get you some pussy and champagne."

Shorty nodded and pulled out the slim tools he'd brought for the night's work: an eight-inch buck knife and a metal mallet he'd picked up at a local hardware store. He took an awkward swing with the mallet and a quick stab with the knife. He was ready.

"Shorty, remember what we told you. You're not gonna kill 'em. Just hurt 'em both real good so they remember never to fuck with us."

Shorty made a disgusted face like he hated being talked down to. "Shit, Dante, I ain't stupid. Just let me do this thing so I can go get me some."

With that Dante nodded and waved his newest recruit toward the stairwell. They let Shorty get a decent lead and then hit street level themselves. Always within sight, he was easy to spot in his black and gold clothing.

They continued to follow as Shorty closed the distance between himself and the young couple. He could now make out their features. The young man wore a pair of faded but stylish jeans and one of those cowboy plaid-looking shirts that were popular. The man looked to be in his twenties, just shy of six feet, and walked with a casual air. He had a medium build. Nothing special. His light brown hair was short and slightly spiked in the front. He looked like a ton of other white boys Shorty saw every day at school. The young man smiled as he talked to the girl whose hand he was holding.

The girl also had light brown hair that she wore straight and that hung just past her shoulders. She was attractive and looked athletic. She wore jeans and form-fitting pink t-shirt. Again, nothing over the top amazing, just normal.

Shorty gauged the distance between himself, the couple, and the alley Dante had appointed as the jump spot. He was twenty feet from the couple. The man and woman were fifty feet from alley. The time was almost right.

As the couple nearly reached the small alley Shorty quickly closed the distance to the couple. The plan was to quickly grab the girl and pull her into the alley. The boyfriend would, of course, follow and try to get her back. Meanwhile, the rest of Dante's crew would close in and seal off the end of the alley and shield the scene from potential onlookers. It would sound and look like a normal post-bar brawl that were common on any night in downtown Nashville.

He could see his soon to be gang brothers swiftly approaching. It was time to act.

Shorty closed the remaining distance from the couple, wrapped his right arm around the waist of the young woman and pulled her into the small alley. She screamed to her fiancé.

"Cal!"

Shorty kept a wary eye on the boyfriend and was surprised to see the young man already following.

Not a problem. His boys would take care of him.

Shorty pulled the now struggling girl farther into the alley and threw her down roughly while simultaneously turning, extracting his weapons, and prepared for the approaching boyfriend.

The young man was five feet away and had a look on his face that Shorty wasn't expecting. Shorty thought the young man would be scared shitless. Instead, his pursuer looked stone cold determined without the smallest trace of fear. *What the fuck?* Shorty thought.

As the final foot between them closed Shorty swung at the man with an overhand chop. The young man ignored the mallet and rushed full steam into Shorty. Both men fell to the ground with the new recruit exposed on the bottom.

Shorty quickly felt the man's hands gripping his head and the man's thumbs found his eyes. *This motherfucker is gonna take out my eyes!* thought a now frantic Shorty.

What Shorty couldn't know what that the young man had realized the trap, although too late, when he glimpsed the remaining gang members block the opening to the alley. His one chance was a full-on frontal assault. Take out the first man, and then see if he could deal with the rest. In the meantime, hopefully his new fiancée could get away and find help.

The man continued to apply pressure as Shorty dropped both weapons and scrambled to free himself. Too late. The would-be victim ripped out both eyeballs as Shorty wailed and clawed at his now empty eye sockets.

The young man grabbed both weapons and hopped back up to his feet.

*One down.* Thought Cal. He had seen and done worse on the battlefields of Afghanistan. Then it was for his country and the survival of his Marines, now it was for the wellbeing of his new fiancé. *Fuck*, he thought.

As he turned to the alley entrance the remaining gang members closed within striking distance. Two moved towards Jessica and Dante and another slowly approached the young man.

"You shouldn't have done that to Shorty, boy. Now you're gonna get something from me." Dante withdrew a shiny silver handgun from his coat pocket and pointed it at Jessica.

Cal stiffened. "You point that thing at me, mother fucker. You wanna fuck with someone, fuck with me."

"OK, boy." Dante swiveled the weapon back to the young man. "I'll fuck with you now."

Dante leveled the gun back to his fiancé and fired four shots into her body.

"No!" Cal screamed in defiance and with knife leading ran the five feet and jumped on the gang banger closest to his now immobile fiancé. The knife plunged into the chest of his target just as Cal simultaneously brought the heavy mallet down on top of the man's head.

As the man fell to the ground Cal planted his feet, pivoted right and backhanded the third gang member with the mallet in the side of the face. He followed the third crew member's descent and followed the initial mallet blow with a deep knife slash across the man's neck. Blood shot up like a geyser and immediately coated Cal's face and chest as he bent over the now dying man.

He turned back towards Dante with a look of total blood-lust and charged. In his mind he knew that unless he took out these last two men, his fiancé would die. That could not happen. How had he survived multiple tours and numerous wounds in the war-torn lands of Afghanistan only to fall prey to these men?

Although his mind raged with bloodlust, his mission remained clear: Kill the enemy.

Closing the short distance to his assailant Dante fired his remaining rounds at the battle raged young man. Six of the eight shots missed wide because Dante was suddenly unnerved by the skill of this supposedly 'normal' white boy. The last two shots hit their target only because the final distance was a mere two feet. One round hit the young man in the chest and one in the shoulder.

Still the young man managed to grab hold of Dante and take him to the ground. A blood-soaked Cal head-butted Dante two times in the nose before the only other remaining gang member pulled him off.

As he was being pulled back Cal tried to turn and face his newest attacker. Instead he fumbled with the blood drenched weapons and staggered back. With his strength fading and the pain from his two bullet wounds increasing, the young man's mind started to fog. *Focus dammit!* he yelled in his head.

He shook his head and turned to see the fourth gang member. What he wouldn't give to have his pistol right now. *Gotta make do*, he thought.

Instead, he hefted the now excruciatingly heavy mallet and heaved it at the fourth man. Instead of watching whether the mallet hit its target, Cal followed right behind, knife blade once again leading, and bowled over his target while plunging the blade into the man's gut.

The man squirmed, screamed and struggled to get away from his attacker. Cal left the gutted gang member and turned to look for Dante. The fearless leader was now half-staggering and half-running towards the opposite end of the alley, glancing over his shoulder as he ran.

Cal suddenly noticed the presence of a quickly growing crowd at the entrance of the alley. He stumbled for a step and fell to his hands and knees.

"Jessica!" he screamed as he crawled towards his fiancé, who was now lying in a large pool of blood. "Jess!"

He reached her side and painfully pulled himself so that his face was next to hers. Her eyes were strangely clear as she looked at him. He'd seen people die in war and by the look of her wounds he was sure Jessica was on her way.

"Hey, baby," Cal whispered. "It's gonna be OK."

Jess smiled. Her voice was weak. "Don't you lie to me, Cal. You know I always know when you lie."

"OK, Jess, but I'm here with you."

"I love you, Cal. I love..."

"Jess? Jess!"

Her breathing stopped and her eyes lost their spark. Cal's world caved in. Nothing mattered anymore. As he faded to blackness, his thoughts were of Jessica and war. Two things he needed and could never seem to avoid.

## VANDERBILT UNIVERSITY HOSPITAL, INTENSIVE CARE UNIT, NASHVILLE, TN

I mages swirled in his mind. The dry air of the open desert. Bloody comrades screaming for help. Friends, family, enemies.

Jessica in a blue gown at the Marine Corps Ball. Jessica walking down the Lawn at the University of Virginia. Jessica crying as he slipped the sparkling engagement ring on her finger. Jessica breathing her last breath.

Jessica, Jessica, Jess...

———

CAL STOKES slowly opened his swollen eyes. His body felt completely immobilized. *What the hell?* he wondered. Slowly and with no small difficulty, he tried to focus on his surroundings. He was obviously in a hospital. The writing on the door still looked like a grayish blob so he decided he'd figure out the particulars later.

He remembered the attack in the alley. He remembered Jess dying. The pain in his heart returned.

When he thought about that last moment with his

dead fiancé, he tried to focus on her beautiful face and her tranquil eyes. He'd always felt that her eyes were what really did him in that first night they'd met six years before. Those beautiful eyes would always haunt him.

As he pondered his misery, the door swung open and a young Hispanic looking hospital staff member walked in.

"I see you're awake," he said. "How you feeling Staff Sergeant?"

Ignoring the question and the comment about his prior military rank, Cal answered with a croak. "Where am I?"

"They brought you over here to Vandy after the attack. You were pretty damn beat up. Haven't seen anything like that since I was in Iraq."

As he talked, the nurse busied himself by taking notes from the machines Cal was hooked up to.

"How long have I been here?" Cal asked.

"About a week. You were full of holes and in critical condition. You got lucky though. The bullets missed anything vital. No permanent damage, mostly blood loss. By the looks of your other scars, this isn't the first time you've spent in a hospital. The docs wanted to keep you sedated for a bit so your body could heal."

"When can I leave?"

The man chuckled. "Just like a Marine. Staff Sergeant, you're not going anywhere for a few days. Why don't you kick back and let us pamper you a bit?"

As the nurse continued around the room in what looked like a practiced habit of checks and rechecks, Cal wondered how he'd found out about his military service. *I guess you can find pretty much anything on the Internet these days. I've gotta get out of here and talk to Jess's parents.*

The man circled around again. "Can I get you anything, Staff Sergeant?"

"Call me Cal. I left that Marine stuff behind. What do I call you?"

"My name is Brian Ramirez. Or you can call me nurse-man."

"You said you were in Iraq. Who were you with?"

"I was with you jarheads. I was a corpsman with 1/2. You were with 3/8, right?"

"Yeah." Cal groaned as he readjusted. "How about I just call you Doc."

"No problem. Takes me back to the days with my platoon. You dumb grunts can never remember anyone's real name. You need anything?"

"I'm good. Thanks, Doc."

Brian nodded and left the room.

Cal was surprised to have a corpsman taking care of him. Maybe he'd been paired with Brian once they found out he'd been in the Marine Corps. Whatever. He just wanted to get out of the hospital.

# OUTSKIRTS OF NASHVILLE, TN

Dante was screaming into his cellphone. "What do you mean that motherfucker's still alive?! I pumped that boy full of lead!" He listened intently as the speaker on the other end of the conversation relayed more information. "Well you tell that bitch she better keep her eye on things and tell me as soon as that fucker gets released!"

Dante stared down at his phone seething with rage. How the hell had everything gone so wrong? A week ago, he'd had a crew of promising members and a highly profitable business. Now he was left with a crew full of worthless bitches.

To make matters worse, the media and the police had picked up on the bloody attack and now Dante was on the run. Never in the same place two nights in a row. He'd done it before down in Louisiana, but this was different. He felt like the whole world was looking for him.

Maybe it was time to head back to New Orleans? No. He had to stay in Nashville and finish what he'd started. Besides, if he went back south he'd be laughed at as he ran back into town hiding from the authorities. He'd worked too hard to let everything go bad. He had too much raw talent.

No. He had to finish things with this damn Marine.

Damn Marine! How the hell could they have known that Shorty was about to attack a Marine hero?!

It was plastered all over the news about how the returning Navy Cross winner and his fiancé had been brutally attacked in the middle of busy downtown Nashville. Local authorities and veterans' groups were in an uproar. Roving bands of retired military and their supporters walked the downtown streets just waiting for provocation.

The Marine veteran had turned into a folk legend in a matter of days. Stories varied as to the exact chain of events from that night (the police were being unusually tight-lipped), but what no one could deny was that somehow this one former Staff Sergeant, in self-defense, had killed three men, blinded a fourth and wounded the only one to escape: Dante West.

What seemed like a simple initiation at one point had now turned into a complete nightmare for Dante and his crew. Just over a week prior his hookers could peddle their wares, his pushers could sell their drugs, and his boys could walk the streets sporting their colors. Now the police had identified the once silent gang. Shorty had helped their efforts by squealing like a pig and unloading anything and everything he knew about Dante and N.O.N.

Other than Dante, the blinded Shorty was the only other gang member to survive Cal Stokes' wrath. Shorty had been taken to the hospital, where he'd been pronounced healthy save the loss of two eyes, and remained under the supervision of the police and hospital staff.

Under very basic interrogation, a scared and defenseless Shorty had divulged the entire plan for the night's attack, including why the couple was picked and who N.O.N. and its members were.

Shorty had outed Dante and his entire crew. It was a

complete and total disaster for Dante who'd spent the time since his move to Nashville carefully choosing new recruits and keeping his base of operations under the radar of the local police and other rival gangs. Now N.O.N. was national news and he'd already felt the pressure from his rivals. Hell, the media had even taken to making fun of the gang's name. Enough was enough. It was time for Dante to take back control. He hadn't worked so hard to let it fall so fast.

He would push the envelope and show that damn Marine how bad things could really get.

## VANDERBILT UNIVERSITY HOSPITAL, NASHVILLE, TN

I t had been two days since Cal had regained consciousness. His mind's sharpness returned, he focused on exceeding his doctor's expectations of recovery so he could get out of the hospital sooner.

His only companion and now friend was the nurse, Brian Ramirez. Over the preceding two days Brian filled Cal in on what was being televised about the investigation into the attack that killed Jessica.

"So, you're telling me they know who led the attack and they still don't have him in jail?" Cal asked.

"Yep, this guy Dante West is supposedly the leader of this little transplanted gang. They say he's a pretty mean sono-fabitch." Brian took a minute to write something down on his clipboard, then continued. "Came up here from New Orleans after Katrina. They interviewed some of his extended family down south and they were all pretty tight-lipped. I think they're afraid of him coming after them. Cops say he was apparently into drugs and running with local gangs by the time he was twelve. Has a long record including attempted murder and battery."

"If they know who he is why can't they find him?"

"The cops I've seen on TV say he's hit the streets. They've got a huge manhunt out for him. Word is the military vets on the police force can't wait to find him and hope he'll go down fighting. Nobody likes the way things went down with your girl."

"Yeah." Cal's voice sounded absent.

Part of him hoped and prayed he would be the one to find that piece of shit. To put a couple rounds into his gut and watch him die might make his despair a little more palatable.

"So, what do you wanna do today?" Brian asked.

"What are you—my nanny now?"

"Let's just say the hospital staff has decided no one else has the patience to deal with a grumpy grunt."

In fact, Cal knew the real reason Brian seemed to be his now constant companion. He had a feeling Brian had requested the crap duty of babysitting him. He'd even heard a heated conversation between Brian and one of the head nurses the previous night. Apparently, it was the end of Brian's shift and the head nurse had pushed him to go home.

Brian had been half yelling, apparently not too worried about who heard him. "If you're so worried about me why don't you go get me a cup of coffee and let me do my job?"

The calming tone of the head nurse's voice was probably a good indication of why she had the job. "Brian, you know we can't pay you for the overtime. Hospital policy is pretty strict on that these days."

"I don't give a shit about the pay," Brian had said. "I'll clock out, but don't tell Staff Sergeant Stokes about it. He's one of my Marines and I'll be damned if he sits here all alone after losing his fiancé. Hell, didn't you hear that even his parents are already dead?"

The head nurse had relented and Brian strolled into Cal's room as if the altercation had never occurred. Cal decided to play along and didn't mention overhearing. Sometimes it was good to have even a swabby corpsman on your side.

"So, what do you wanna do today?" Brian repeated.

"Let's get some of this rehab out of the way. I've gotta get the hell out of this place."

"Alright, Cal, but don't forget what your doctor said. You've gotta take it easy for a while."

"Yeah, yeah." Cal looked up at his nurse. "Look, I've been through this shit before and I'm really getting sick of the crappy hospital food. I'd rather be eating MREs right now."

Brian chuckled. "My ass. All right, Marine. Let me go get a wheelchair and we'll head down to physical therapy."

As Brian left to retrieve the wheelchair Cal started to pull himself up and out from under the covers. He was still in intense pain. Hell, taking a couple shots was never a vacation. Luckily that dumbshit gang-banger had missed anything too vital. Apparently the EMT's and ER staff had patched him up pretty quickly. It also hadn't hurt that he had been shot at point blank range. Better than taking a round at 100 yards.

By the time Brian returned Cal had managed to work up a sweat but had slipped his legs over the side of the bed and was in the process of putting on his hospital slippers.

Shit, rehab was going to be a real bitch.

# HEADQUARTERS MARINE CORPS, NAVY ANNEX, WASHINGTON, DC

The Marine Captain had some time between phone calls so he decided to peruse the day's news on the internet. *"The Drudge Report"* was set at his homepage and he did a quick scan of the day's top stories. Capt. Andrews – Andy to his friends – was trying to kill time in an otherwise boring day. He paused a quarter of the way down:

*Navy Cross Marine Loses Fiancé in Bloody Gang Attack, Hero Kills Four with Bare Hands*

Despite the recent conflicts overseas there still weren't many living Marines wearing the nation's second highest award for gallantry in battle. He knew two personally.

The Captain clicked on the article link and started reading:

*In a rare act of restraint, Nashville police have somehow kept a recent bloody attack out of the local and national spotlight. What was initially reported as a mugging gone wrong now seems to be much more.*

This publication initially reported that an unidentified man and woman were mugged on Second Avenue in downtown Nashville. The man has been identified as former Marine Staff Sergeant Calvin Stokes. Through our contacts in the military establishment it has been confirmed that SSgt Stokes was honorably discharged from the Marine Corps earlier this year. Even more interesting is that SSgt Stokes is a bonified hero having received the Navy Cross for gallantry on the battlefield in Afghanistan.

Our next segment will have the award citation in its entirety. Our sources have been able to tell us that SSgt Stokes was awarded the Navy Cross for saving the majority of his platoon after being ambushed. Still unconfirmed is whether SSgt Stokes also killed twenty enemy combatants during the firefight.

What we can tell you about this most recent attack in Downtown Nashville is that SSgt Stokes's fiancé, Jessica Warren of Franklin, TN, was killed along with four members of the local gang N.O.N. Still unconfirmed is the status of a fifth man who was apparently blinded during the downtown battle.

Police confirmed that SSgt Stokes is the man responsible for killing the four men, blinding the fifth and wounded a sixth. The method of wounding is still unconfirmed but initial reports from eye witnesses point toward SSgt Stokes using his hands and a knife for the majority of the attack.

SSgt Stokes is currently being held in the intensive care ward of Vanderbilt University Hospital. He is said to be in stable condition.

We do know that local police and the Tennessee Bureau of Investigation (TBI) are searching for Dante West, the alleged leader and founder of N.O.N.

All this raises the question: What happened in that alley?

This publication is still sifting through various eye witness accounts and speculation. If you have any additional information on the attack please contact us through our website or 24-hour hotline.

"Shit," Andy muttered.

He picked up the phone on his desk and dialed information.

"Vanderbilt University Hospital in Nashville, Tennessee, please."

The phone next to his bed rang. Cal picked it up and answered by habit. "Stokes."

Brian was on the other end. "Hey, Cal. You've got a call from Headquarters Marine Corps. Some Captain says he know you. You want me to tell him you're out for a stroll?"

"He mention what his name was?"

"Yeah. Captain Andrews."

Cal took a deep breath. "You can patch him through."

Capt. Andrews had been Cal's platoon commander on his last two tours in Afghanistan. Capt. Andrews had then been First Lieutenant Andrews and one of the Marines Cal had saved in that damned ambush. Andrews had reciprocated on their next tour by carrying a badly wounded Stokes, then a Sergeant, out of another firefight. For that action, and for saving a bunch of Marines and Afghan soldiers, Capt. Andrews had later also been awarded a Navy Cross.

The phone clicked through and Cal heard the voice of his former platoon commander. "You there, Stokes?"

"Hey, Captain," Cal answered. "Didn't know they had you

riding a desk at Headquarters. You playing butler for the Commandant?"

"Very funny, Stokes. No, they've got me sitting here waiting to take a platoon at Eighth and I. And didn't I tell you not to call me Sir or Captain? We've been through too much for that, brother. Call me Andy."

Capt. Andrews's real name was Bartholomew G. Andrews. For obvious reason he didn't want to be called Bartholomew or the even more heinous Bart. As a result, all his friends shortened his last name and just called him Andy.

"Hard for me to turn that switch off, *Andy*."

Andy paused for a beat. "Just heard about what happened to Jess. I can't tell you how sorry I am, Cal. If I'd known sooner I would've flown out. Anything I can do?"

"You think you can get the Commandant to get me out of this hospital?"

"What kinda shape you in?"

Cal looked down at his body, which was propped up in the hospital bed. "Not too bad. Up and walking. Don't really need to be here."

"If you're still anything like you were a couple years ago that probably means you're pretty beat up," Andy said. "Weren't you the dumbass that snuck out of that hospital in Germany and tried to stowaway in that C-130 on its way back to Afghanistan dressed like a Navy nurse?"

"You know why I did that, Andy. I had to get back to my Marines."

"I know, I know." Andy sighed. "I just want to make sure you take care of yourself. According to the papers, you got into some real shit."

"Thanks, Sir. I just want to get as far away from this place as I can."

"You talk to the police yet?"

"Yeah, they sent in some former Army guy. He was all

right. Asked me some basic questions and didn't press too much. If anything, it looks like the cops here in Nashville take care of the military."

"Yeah, that's what I'd heard too. Anybody giving you a hard time?"

Cal thought back to earlier in the week. "Had some random calls from reporters but I've got a pretty good former corpsman that screens the calls for me."

"He the guy I just talked to?"

"Yeah. Pretty good guy. Speaking of which, could you do me a favor and do a little digging on him?"

"I thought you said he was a good guy."

"It's not that. But you know me. Never hurts to have a little extra intel."

"No problem," Andy said. "One of the perks of being close to the puzzle palace is that I can get the scoop on almost anyone. What's the doc's name?"

Cal told him what he knew about Brian, which wasn't much.

"Give me a few minutes and I'll call you back."

The line went dead and Cal hung up as well. Cal mulled over the conversation.

So, Capt. Andrews was at Headquarters Marine Corps. Large probability that they got him to make that move kicking and screaming. The good Captain might not look like much, around five feet nine inches, but he was a helluva shot and knew how to take care of his Marines. Most people thought he was a candyass when they first met him because he looked barely twenty-one, but the man was a natural leader. Under the surface lurked a coldly calculating mind not unlike Cal's. Maybe that's why they'd gotten along.

His mind ticked back the seconds, then the minutes, then hours and days and years, back to when he first met then Second Lieutenant Andrews...

# ANDY

*C*orporal Stokes sat at the duty desk counting down the minutes to midnight. This was the much-loved twenty-four-hour duty on a prime Friday night in July. He had a list of junior officers that were supposed to report in to the battalion from the Infantry Officers Course by 23:59. All of the four reported in at various times during the day except one: a 2ndLt. Bartholomew Andrews.

*Bartholomew, huh? Probably some Naval Academy weenie.*

The Gunnery Sergeant assigned as the duty officer was a real prick and wanted to be woken up as soon as each officer reported in. It didn't have to be that way, but this particular Gunny, a GySgt. Remer, got a kick out of giving young officers grief when they reported in.

Cal knew why too. The prick had been dumped by two Company Commanders for doing a shitty job as Company Gunny. Now he was assigned to the S-3 shop as some assistant to the assistant's assistant. Basically, the Battalion staff was biding its time until they could dump the waste of space onto another Battalion or get him kicked out of the Corps altogether. Remer loved to abuse any power granted to him by the Marine Corps, even the limited power of the Officer of the Day. Guys like that tend to relish OOD duty as their time to shine.

He'd seen the guy earlier that week, pacing before two unfortunate new arrivals like a rooster with a hard-on. He shoved his pecking beak into one poor officer's face.

"Lieutenant, where are your written orders?"

He liked to say 'Lieutenant' like it was some obscenity he'd been whipped for in Catholic school.

"In my car." The poor guy was shaking.

"In your car?" screamed the Gunny. "Is your car pulling duty now, Lieutenant?"

"No, Gunnery Sergeant!" The young officer was bubbling with unease now.

"You are to carry your written orders at all times like they're nailed to your chest, you understand, Lieutenant?"

"Yes, Gunnery Sergeant!" There was a slight whine in the officer's tone now, like a banshee who'd lost its voice.

"Yes? So, you agree with me?"

"Yes, Gunnery Sergeant!"

"Then why don't you have them with you?"

The officer's jaw jittered for a moment. "I—"

"I what? You gonna start giving me a bunch of excuses, Lieutenant?"

"No, Gunnery Sergeant!"

"Here's what I need, what the Marine Corps needs. I need you to sprint back to your car right now, you understand, Lieutenant?"

"Yes, Gunnery Sergeant!"

"I want you to run like the devil himself is about to rape your mama, and bring me back those written orders, Lieutenant."

"Yes, Gunnery Sergeant!"

"You think you're special, Lieutenant, cuz the Corps doesn't have room for special cases."

"No, Gunnery Sergeant!"

"You think you don't need written orders?"

"No, Gunnery Sergeant!"

"I want you back here in under two minutes or I *will* call the Battalion Commander and let him deal with you." It was said conversationally, like Remer didn't care, but the threat was as plain as the grass is green.

After this lovely exchange, the officer turned and ran. Cal saw the smirk appear on the Remer's smug, self-satisfied face. Then the prick actually laughed out loud.

Cal wasn't looking forward to the last guy, Andrews, getting there. The second lieutenant had ten more minutes. It was also obvious that the Gunny was saving the best for last.

"Bartholomew," the Gunny sneered to Cal. "Anyone with a name like that is just begging to be messed with."

No, Bartholomew wasn't Cal's first choice to name a kid, but at least he had the decency o keep that fact to himself, and not make it the justification for some petty abuse to make himself feel like he had a pair.

At five minutes before midnight, 2ndLt Andrews walked into the duty shack with his orders ready. He looked squared away and fairly at ease. Most new Marines Cal had seen checking in to their first unit tended to be more than a little nervous. This young officer didn't seem to have that problem.

"Checkin' in, Corporal."

Cal looked up at him. "Roger that, sir. If I can just get your orders. I've gotta go get the duty officer to get you logged in."

"No problem."

Cpl. Stokes got up and walked smartly into the next room.

which was used for the duty officer and his clerks as a sleeping area.

"Hey, Gunny. That last Lieutenant just walked in."

Remer opened his eyes with what looked like a mixture of disdain and excitement. Yep, he was gonna give the new guy some kinda shit alright.

Cal waited as the Gunny took his time putting his utility blouse back on and donning his web belt with pistol. Cpl. Stokes was surprised the guy could even fit into any issued gear. The Gunny's belly gave his buttons a workout.

Finally ready, Cal followed Remer back into the duty shack. Not two steps through the door, the Gunny started in.

"You Lieutenant Andrews?"

"That's me, Gunny," Andy said. "Just checkin' in."

"I'd appreciate it if you called me 'Gunnery Sergeant,' Sir."

That was one of Remer's favorite lines. Get the young officers off-balance from the get-go.

"Sorry, Gunnery Sergeant. Didn't mean any disrespect." Lt. Andrews responded without the obligatory flush of embarrassment. Cal couldn't yet put his finger on it, but he didn't think this baby-faced butter bar was even close to being a candyass.

"Says here you were supposed to report in by 2359, Lieutenant. It's now 0002."

Andy nodded toward Cal. "As I'm sure Cpl. Stokes will tell you, I stepped in and reported at 2355."

The Gunny smirked. "Well, sir, that's not really my concern. The point is when I put you in the logbook, you'll be reporting in late. Helluva way to start your tour with this fine battalion."

Just then Cal caught the look of cold anger flash across the eyes of the young officer. Then just like that, it was gone. This guy was no candyass.

From the look on the Remer's face, it was obvious he'd

missed the warning sign. Cal decided to step in. "Hey, Gunny, the Lieutenant's right. He checked in right at 2355. I wrote it right here in my own log."

"You shut your mouth, Corporal," Remer snapped. "Looks like you'll have to come back tomorrow morning to meet with the Battalion XO, sir. He likes to come in Saturday morning and check-in with the OOD to see who fucked up the night before."

Surprisingly, Lt. Andrews still stood in front of the duty desk with a look of complete calm. "OK, Gunnery Sergeant. Why don't you just pick up that phone and call the XO right now. If I'm gonna get my ass chewed, I'd rather not wait until tomorrow."

Visibly confused, Remer paused to think about that most unexpected request. Calling the Executive Officer would put *his* ass in a crack, and he was all about keeping his ass out of cracks no matter whom he had to blame to take the fall for him.

Remer's voice became condescendingly soothing. "Well, Lieutenant, I don't think it's appropriate to call the XO at this hour. Why don't you just come back in the morning and I'm sure everything will be fine."

"I think I'll take my chances, Gunnery Sergeant. Why don't you give me his number and I'll call him right now on my handy-dandy cellphone."

The corner of Remer's mouth twitched, barely imperceptibly. He was starting to lose his patience. "Now, Sir, that's really not how things are done around here."

Andy's voice was suddenly commanding. "Well then how are they done around here, *Gunnery Sergeant?* It's obvious you get your rocks off shitting on us new guys. Get the damn XO on the phone and we'll get this done. *Now.*"

The placid demeanor had evaporated and a look of calm fury now radiated from the young officer's face. And by the look on Remer's face, the shitbird Gunny was finally getting the point: He'd messed with the wrong guy. He could either back down or push forward. Cal hoped he'd pick the first option.

The Gunny sneered in Andy's direction. "Now look here, *Lioutenant* I don't appreciate—"

"Get on your feet, Marine!" Andy bellowed. "You stand at attention when you talk to me, *Gunnery Sergeant*."

It therefore came as a complete surprise to Cal when the Gunny jumped out of his seat and popped to attention. *Holy shit!* What was going on?

"Now as I see it," said Andy, "you have two choices. Number One, you log me as reporting in at 23:55. Number Two, you get the Battalion XO on the phone right now and he can resolve the issue. What's it gonna be, Gunnery Sergeant?"

Remer stammered as he answered the other man. "I'm just trying to do things by the book, but I think we can trust your word that you reported in at that time."

"Sir."

"Excuse me?"

"I said you call me 'Sir'," Andy said. "I'm only asking for the same respect you so kindly asked of me."

"Yes, Sir," the Gunny said.

"Alright, let's get this done so Cpl. Stokes can get some rack time. He's looking a little sickly."

As Remer leaned over to begin his entry in the duty logbook, Lt. Andrews gave Cal a quick wink and a mischievous half smile. It was the same smile he'd see years later on the side of some God-forsaken mountain in Afghanistan as he and Lt. Andrews prepared to rush an enemy position by themselves.

And it was that first meeting, and the look in that young

officer's eyes, that made Cpl. Stokes think he never wanted to get on the officer's bad side.

———

## VANDERBILT UNIVERSITY HOSPITAL, NASHVILLE, TN

The bedside phone rang again a couple minutes later. Cal picked it up on the first ring. "Stokes."

It was Brian. "Cal, I've got Capt. Andrews on the phone again."

"Put him through."

"You there, Stokes?" Andy asked.

"Yes, sir."

"I got some info on your corpsman."

Cal shifted into a more comfortable position. "What'd you find?"

"Says here that he served with 1/2 during the initial invasion of Iraq. He got to be part of that big mess in An'Nasiriyah. Hold on a minute."

Cal heard mouse clicks on the other end.

"Well, well," said Andy, "looks like you've got yourself a brother there, Marine."

"What do you mean?"

"This record says that Hospital Corpsman First Class Brian Ramirez is a multiple award winner. Won a Bronze Star in Iraq then a Silver Star in Afghanistan. Hmmm... the first was for dragging some of his Marines out of a burning AAV. Says he got some pretty bad burns himself. The Silver Star citation says that this kid not only saved ten of his Marines' lives, but that he also took up a couple M-16s and killed a few bad guys."

"No shit?"

"No shit."

"Impressive. Well, at least I know now."

"Need anything else?" Andy asked.

"Unless you can get me out of here, I'm good."

"Wish I could, buddy. I'll be in touch."

The line went dead. Cal replaced the receiver and laid back in his bed.

So, Brian was a warrior. *Interesting.*

———

A FEW MINUTES later Doc Ramirez came in to check on Cal.

"What do you want for dinner tonight?" Brian asked.

"You didn't tell me about your Bronze and Silver Stars."

Brian quirked an eyebrow. "You didn't tell me about your Navy Cross."

"Fair enough. I'd give that thing back just to have my guys alive right now."

"Me too. Now, what do you want for dinner? Chicken or mystery meat?"

Cal snorted. "I'll take the chicken."

As Brian nodded and left the room Cal thought about the quick conversation. It was rare to find a medal recipient who bragged about their award. Most just wanted to be left alone. He'd seen guys give their medals away as soon as they'd been received rather than once again re-live the memory of their dying comrades. Funny that heroes come in all shapes and sizes, but the true heroes are almost always silent about their accolades.

Brian returned balancing a cafeteria tray with a domed cover. The faint smell of roasted chicken wafted toward Cal.

"Hey, Doc, wondering if you could do me a favor."

Brian set the meal down on the table next to Cal. "What's that?"

"I was wondering if you could swing by my place on your way home and pick up a couple things for me."

"You have a place here in Nashville?"

"Yeah. I've got a little condo down in the Gulch."

"Sure, no problem. You got your keys?"

"You actually won't need any. There are two keypads: one at the building entrance and one at my unit. I'll just give you the codes."

"Ew, fancy. What are you some rich kid?" A brief look of anger passed across Cal's eyes and Brian backtracked. "Did I say something wrong?"

Cal shook his head. "Don't worry about it. Can you run by there tonight?"

"No problem. I get off at seven. I'll run by after that. What do you need me to pick up?"

"Call me when you get there and I'll walk you through it. Won't be easy to find without me telling you."

Brian's eyebrow rose. What was this Marine having him deliver? He'd find out soon enough. He was *pretty sure* he could trust Cal Stokes.

## GULCH DISTRICT, NASHVILLE, TENNESSEE

Compared to Brian's tiny apartment, Cal's building was the Taj Mahal. He pulled up to the side of the high-rise condo. *What the hell does this guy do for a living now that he's out of the Corps?*

He got out of his car and walked to the building's entrance. A collection of mixed citizenry walked the sidewalks on either side of the street. Brian could see at least two high-end restaurants within a block of Cal's building. Looked like the area was really taking off. He'd heard that there'd been a lot of redevelopment in the Gulch in recent years. Not a bad place to live.

The passcode Cal gave him got him in the glassed front door. A few steps inside he could see what appeared to be a receptionist glancing over at him. As he got closer, she perked up.

"Can I help you, sir?"

"I'm good. Just picking up some things for my buddy in the hospital."

She looked startled and came out of her seat.

"Is that Cal you're talking about?"

"It is."

"Oh my God, is he OK? We heard all about it on the news! He's such a nice guy. When is he coming home?"

"I can't say for sure, but he's doing a lot better. I'll tell him you asked about him..."

"Irene."

"I'll tell him you asked about him, Irene."

Brian exited the elevator on the 23rd floor. There were only two doors visible along the hallway. Cal's was almost directly across from the elevator.

He quickly punched in Cal's code and entered the condo. Despite its opening smoothly, he could feel the weight of the door. Standard issue or an upgrade Cal had installed? *Curious.* The thing reminded him of some of the armored vehicles in the Corps.

By habit he turned around swiftly to lock the door and deadbolt it. No deadbolt. There were, however, two buttons; one about two feet above the door handle and one two feet below. He pressed the button above the handle and heard a mechanical scrape as the deadbolt engaged. He did the same with the lower button then turned to get his bearings.

Even the lobby downstairs hadn't prepared him for this.

What was visible of the unit was almost completely open. You could see the living and dining area from the kitchen. It looked like there was another hallway leading to the bedroom.

The furniture looked new and modern in a Spartan way. Color accents here and there but mostly clean lines and polished stainless steel.

He hadn't met many enlisted guys with a place like this. Once again, he wondered what Cal's whole story was.

What really took his breath away was the view. One whole wall consisted of windows that faced the Nashville skyline. At this time of night, he could see the city clearly.

He pulled out his phone and dialed the hospital switch-board. Seconds later he was connected to Cal's room.

"You get in OK?" Cal asked.

"Yeah. You said you had a little condo in the Gulch. I wasn't expecting Superman's Fortress of Solitude."

"Where are you standing right now?"

"I'm in your living room."

"OK. Head down the hallway toward my bedroom in the back."

"Got it." Brian made his way toward the hallway. Walking into the bedroom he noticed the pictures on the wall. Cal and his fiancée in every shot. *Poor bastard.* "Alright. I'm in your bedroom."

"Go over to my closet and open the doors."

Brian pulled open the two doors, peered inside the huge walk-in, and switched on the light. The closet felt as big as his apartment.

After a couple seconds' pause, Cal continued. "Go to the back of the closet and open the panels of the built-in armoire."

"Done."

"Now take out the bottom right drawer."

Brian put a hand on the handle but didn't pull on it. "You mean open it?"

"No. Take the whole thing out and put it on the floor."

"Now feel along the right side of where you took the drawer out," Cal said. You should feel a button about the size of a dime. Press it and step back."

He suddenly had the nagging sense that he wasn't going to like what was coming next. This was obviously a compart-ment for some kind of secret stash. Drugs, or something worse.

With some trepidation, he pressed the button and heard a mechanical click. He could now see that the interior of the wardrobe had moved forward a bit. There appeared to be a seam in the middle.

"All right, now open the panels. Once you get that open there's a separate light switch inside."

Brian pulled the two heavy panels apart and stepped back. Well, it was definitely a secret stash. Just not the kind Brian had imagined.

Neatly held in racks, and now lit by the interior light, was a bottom row of an assorted number of rifles. The top row was half pistols of varying calibers and half full of other gear like knives, GPS, compass and survival gear.

*What the hell?* thought Brian. *This Marine is ready for war.*

"Grab the first pistol on the top left," Cal said. "Should be my Beretta nine mil. Grab the one next to that too: the forty-five caliber Springfield XD."

Brian shook his head but didn't move. "Hey, man, I can't bring these things back to the hospital. Administration tends to frown on personal arsenals."

"Look, Doc. I know I'm asking a lot on this one but I need your help. You should know me well enough by now to understand that I don't like asking for help."

Brian laughed. "Saw a small glimpse of that the other day when you refused my help getting up to take a piss and landed flat on your face."

Cal sighed, like the memory was a sharp pain in his side. "Yeah, I know. But look, I just have this funny feeling and I want to be prepared. You ever get that feeling in your gut while in the field that something bad was gonna happen?"

"Of course, but, Cal, this is different. You're not in the field and you're surrounded by trained hospital security staff. Not to mention the local cops are always stopping by to see how you're doing."

"You're right," Cal said slowly, "but I thought the same thing about taking Jess out to dinner at a seemingly safe downtown restaurant." Cal let that sink in for a couple seconds and continued. "You know I wouldn't let you take the heat for this. If anyone finds it on me I'll blame it on myself. Thing is, the minute I walk out of that hospital I'll need to have some protection of my own."

Brian's stomach was uneasy. He trusted Cal, but the thought of bringing loaded weapons into the hospital still did not sit well with him. Worst case, he could get fired *and* thrown in jail. He liked his job at Vanderbilt and wasn't planning on leaving anytime soon.

On the other hand, whether a new friend or not, Cal Stokes was his brother-in-arms, a fellow warrior that upheld the highest standards of the military establishment. He knew deep down that Cal would never let him take the fall.

*In for a penny, in for a pound.*

"OK," he conceded. "You said the Beretta and the Springfield. Anything else?"

Cal went on to ask for a couple boxes of ammunition and one of his knives from the top row. Then he instructed Brian to grab one of his gym bags from the front of the closet, fill it with some random clothing and hide the weapons inside.

Brian put the phone down and grabbed the first pistol, reflexively ejecting the full magazine and checking the chamber. *Fully loaded. Just like a Marine.*

The next pistol was the same. With both magazine reinserted he stuffed each into a separate pair of boxer briefs. Next, he grabbed two boxes of ammunition: one of 9mm and one of 45 cal. He finished by hiding the knife in a pair of socks and loading some workout pants, shirts and sweatshirts on top.

Mission completed, he picked the phone back up. "Anything else you need?"

"Yeah. Grab my cell phone. I think it's either on the

kitchen counter or on my nightstand. Thanks again for doing this, Doc."

"Yeah, yeah. You just make sure that if we get sent to jail you're the one that gets to bunk with Bubba."

Cal chuckled. "You got it. I'll see you in the morning."

Brian put his phone back in his coat pocket, picked up the gym bag, now laden with a small arsenal, and took it out into the bedroom and laid it on the bed. He went back into the closet, closed the hidden panels, replaced the drawer, and re-sealed the armoire.

He found Cal's cell phone on the night stand. The thought occurred to him that it was strange how Cal didn't have it with him that night. Didn't most people carry their cell phones everywhere?

He did one final sweep of the condo. Pausing by the nightstand, he grabbed the photograph of Cal and Jessica. It was a portrait of the couple sitting on the edge of a dock at some lake. They looked happy.

With the small picture frame now wrapped in a t-shirt and safely packed in the full gym bag, he headed for the door.

———

BRIAN DECIDED on the way back down to the lobby not to wait until the next morning to get the weapons back to Cal. The night staff at the hospital was lighter and going in through the staff entrance would attract less scrutiny.

He waved to Irene as he went by.

"You tell Cal that we want to know as soon as he's getting out," she said, her voice obnoxiously bubbly. "Maybe we can throw him a little party when he gets back."

"Hope I'm invited," he replied.

It was small talk. The last thing Cal would want coming home was a cocktail party. Guys like Cal didn't want or need that kind of attention. Better to be among close friends or, even better, with a couple Marine buddies drinking beer and swapping sea stories.

He'd tell Cal that the girl had said hello but also warn him about the possibility of a homecoming fiesta. The idea triggered an uncomfortable memory lodged in the back of his brain.

His parents had thrown him a surprise welcome home party once, when he'd returned from overseas. By then, unbeknownst to him, the Navy had already informed the Ramirez family of Brian's valor in battle. His parents decided the best way to convey their pride was to show off their son to a bunch of friends and a few neighbors Brian didn't even know.

He still remembered the look of devastation on his mother's face as he'd screamed at her for throwing the party. She'd left the room crying. Somehow, his father diplomatically ushered the guests out of the house.

Looking back now, his soul ached at the memory of his behavior. It wasn't their fault. His parents were not raised in a military family. They had no idea what it was like to serve in the armed forces. To them it was all parades and a clean-shaven son returning home with apple cheeks and great posture. They just wanted to celebrate their son the hero, to honor Brian in the only way they knew how.

The last thing he wanted was public recognition for acts of gallantry. He didn't even want the awards they'd given him. He just wanted his Marines back.

In time, he'd managed to explain this to his parents. His mother and father loved their only son, evidenced by how hard they worked to understand what he'd been through, realizing that there might never be a right time for him to tell them the whole story.

He'd seen other friends return to similar homecomings, families that had not understood their need for privacy. It was never a good thing. Such breaches of personal space tended to wear out familial bonds, as if no one in the family spoke the same language, causing resentments over a small matter of communication.

That was a problem with serving in the military. The only ones who understand what you've gone through are those who've served as well.

————

FIFTEEN MINUTES LATER, he pulled into the staff parking lot and headed through the staff entrance carrying Cal's things. Security presence was scarce, mainly because most of the doors were locked, only accessible by key-card at this time of night.

He was back in Cal's room in five minutes.

"Hey, doc, I wasn't expecting you back until tomorrow morning."

"Yeah, well, I didn't really want to be lugging around your arsenal for the next twelve hours."

"Thanks again for going. I won't forget it." Cal's eyes were sincere.

"Yeah, yeah. Just don't let anybody see it. It's my ass if the Marine I've been assigned to gets caught with all that gear. Just be careful, OK, Cal?"

Cal nodded and struggled out of bed to grab the gym bag. "Hey, Doc, you wanna do me a favor and go watch the door for me?"

"Sure."

Brian walked over to the door and leaned against it, keeping an eye at the window slit while Cal unpacked the bag.

The first item he pulled out was the framed picture of

him and Jess. He stared down at the picture and touched Jess's face.

Maybe bringing the photo wasn't the best idea. There was something terrible in the Marine's eyes. They watered, as if the pent-up grief was about to overwhelm his resolve.

Something in the man's face changed. His jaw stiffened. Brian heard the sharp intake of breath through the nose. Cal's body straightened as he reverently placed the picture frame on the side table. The whole series of bodily motions, which took all of eight seconds, conveyed a single, powerful decision: *I'm not gonna do this now dammit.*

Next, Cal checked the weapons to make sure they were loaded and ready. Then he took both guns, loaded each into one of his white socks, and stuffed them back into the bag along with the knife.

The Marine had a conspiratorial grin on his face. "The dangerous stuff is back in the bag, Doc. Have a seat if you want to stick around."

Brian narrowed his eyes at him. "Stick around for what?"

"You'll see. I've just got a feeling."

Cal grabbed his cell phone, sat on the edge of the bed and started scrolling through the phone's touch screen. He shook his head and mumbled, "A shit-ton of voicemails."

Brian moved up next to Cal and looked down at the phone. Cal clicked a small camera icon on the home screen and entered a nine-digit pass code. Video footage appeared in a series of scrollable files.

He couldn't believe it. Cal was scrolling through videos taken at his condo.

"Hey, is that me?"

"Yep. I'm starting with the most recent and moving back. I've got these things rigged so that they're motion sensitive. Got 'em hidden pretty well in each room. Bet you didn't see them, did you?"

Brian shook his head. "Why do you have all that surveillance gear up? Speaking of which, what's with the armor-plated door and access code add-on?"

"I thought you might pick up on that. You're not as dumb as you look, swabby." Brian rolled his eyes as Cal continued. "The video surveillance gear is actually through a local security company. Nothing too fancy. I had it installed just as a precaution. I've found you can never be too safe. I usually turn it off while I'm there so I don't waste space filming myself in underwear."

He turned the phone so Brian could get a better picture. "See, here's you getting to my front door. The next camera picks you up coming into the foyer, et cetera."

"Pretty cool."

"Yeah, my dad was in the security business. I guess I picked up on some of his habits."

Brian added that tidbit about Cal's dad to the back of his brain for inquiry at a later date. A family security business would definitely explain the vault and arsenal at Cal's place.

"So, what are you looking for?" Brian asked. "Just want to make sure I wasn't rifling through your panty drawer?"

"Just want to see if anyone else made a visit." Cal sounded distracted.

As Brian watched, Cal fast-forwarded through the footage. He saw the front door's exterior camera pickup residents walking by Cal's unit. After a couple minutes of forwarding Cal stopped. "Hmmm. Looks like Irene stopped by."

"Hey, isn't that the girl from the front desk?"

"Yeah, her name's Irene. Nice enough girl, but kind of nosy."

"She said to say hello by the way."

Cal ignored the comment and kept his eyes on the small screen. At first, Irene looked like she was knocking on the door. Then she pulled out her cell phone and made a phone call while standing right in front of Cal's door. She looked nervous. The video didn't have sound but Brian got the impression that Irene didn't like what she was hearing from the other end.

Finally, she hung up the phone and put it back in her pocket. She approached the door again and it looked like she was entering a pass code to get in.

The next frame showed Irene stepping into Cal's foyer just as they'd seen a few minutes before with Brian's visit to the condo.

Cal sat up. "What the hell is she doing?"

"Maybe checking to make sure you hadn't left the stove on or something."

"Doubt it. The building staff isn't supposed to enter the private residences unless there's an emergency. Plus, she doesn't know I have cameras installed."

As they both watched, Irene made her way through the living area and kitchen. She seemed to be looking for something. She paused to open random drawers and peer inside. Nothing she saw seemed to be of much interest.

"What the hell is she looking for?" Cal said.

Irene moved from the living area to Cal's bedroom. She opened the drawers on the bedside table and picked up Cal's cell phone out of the charging cradle. It looked like she'd pressed the unlock button on the phone but without the unlock code she quickly grew frustrated and put the phone back down in its charger.

She moved to the other side of the bed and picked up a small package that appeared to have already been opened.

Cal clenched his teeth. "Tell me that package was there when you went by, Doc."

"Yeah it was there, I think. What is it?"

"Just a little engagement gift from Jess's parents."

Peering back down at the phone, they watched as Irene set the package down and advanced her search.

The woman did a quick scan of the bedroom closet then headed back towards the main living area. She looked around one more time then left through the front door.

"Irene's gonna have a little explaining to do."

Brian crossed his arms. "You wanna tell me what's going on?"

"The less you know the better, Doc. I already exposed you by having you go by my place. Don't worry about it. I'll take care of it."

Brian scoffed. "Look, brother, I don't know what the hell's going on but I do know that you're in no condition to be doing much of anything. So, if you need help, I'm here."

Cal stared at Brian for a moment and nodded. "If this goes to shit in a couple days don't say I didn't warn you."

"Sounds like what my platoon sergeant said to me after I volunteered for that ambushed patrol."

"Didn't you learn never to volunteer for anything in the military, Doc?"

"Yeah." Brian smiled. "I guess I'm just a slow learner."

"OK. Here's what I think." Cal looked back down at the video. "That guy that attacked me, Dante West, isn't done with me yet. I'll bet he's not happy about what I did to his crew. He's also pissed that I messed up his face."

"You think he's coming after you?"

"Yeah."

"Why not your family?"

"All my family's dead. I'm all that's left."

Brian's eyebrows knit together. "What about all those phone calls you've been getting? The ones you don't want to take?"

"They're guys with my dad's company. I'll deal with them later."

"Hey, man, I know this whole situation sucks but you've gotta talk to someone. You can't just hole up here and pretend the outside world doesn't exist. I'll bet those guys are worried about you."

Cal stared at Brian for a minute then nodded. "I'll call them in a minute. Can you do me another favor?"

"What now? You want me to go break someone out of jail?"

"No, smartass. Can you go get me some coffee? I think this is gonna be a long night."

Brian agreed and left the room. As he made his way to the cafeteria, he thought about what Cal had said about his family. He was sure Jess's family had tried to see Cal, only the stubborn Marine had refused any and all visitors.

He also had a stack of messages from various callers all waiting to check on Cal's condition. Brian had kept tight-lipped until now, but he knew that would have to change. In order for Cal to make a full physical and, more importantly, mental recovery after losing Jess, he'd have to let his friends help. As a nurse and corpsman, Brian had seen a lot of troops clam up and refuse treatment. Some never made it back to reality. Others drowned their demons in booze and drugs.

Cal Stokes didn't seem like the type to go off the deep end, but having a strong support system would still be crucial in getting back to full form. If Cal didn't make the calls himself, Brian would make some for him.

There's no other decision to make when your brother falls. You pick him up. That's that.

# VANDERBILT UNIVERSITY HOSPITAL, NASHVILLE, TN

Cal Stokes stared at the ceiling. He had the urge to chuck pencils at it. A moment later, Brian entered clutching a stack of papers in one hand and a cheap Styrofoam cup in the other. At least it was hot.

"Forgot I'd stashed this back at the nurse's station. Phone messages."

Cal grabbed the coffee and the inch-thick stack of messages. "This many people called for me?"

"Yeah. You must be famous or something." Brian chuckled. "I put what sounded like friends and family on the top and left the reporters and weirdos on the bottom."

Brian left the room and Cal looked down at the top message. It was from Jess's dad, Frank, earlier that morning. He thumbed through the rest and saw that Frank had called at least three times a day. Under those messages, was a bunch from his dad's company: old friends checking to make sure he was OK. *Sorry guys but you'll have to wait a little bit longer.*

He took a deep breath, picked up his cell phone and dialed Jess's parents' number by memory. Frank picked up after the first ring.

"Cal?"

"Hey, Frank... I... I..."

All his experience in tactical maneuvers, and yet nothing prepared him for this moment.

"I know, son..."

Suddenly, Jess's old man was real. He wasn't just some piece of collateral damage to be figured into the equation after the fact. He saw the man's kind eyes in his head. Remembered the plainspoken way he had about him. The way he called him 'son'.

Cal could hear the muted crying on the other end, and that's when he lost it. "Frank, I am so sorry... so sorry... tried... sorry..."

Something had crawled inside the hole in his life and poked at its walls with a dagger. It began with a soft sob, and a feeble attempt to suppress it. All decorum went out the window and he broke, dropping the phone into his lap.

The tears and the sobs continued for a few minutes.

This was grief. This was every loss magnified, replayed. This was the dagger poking, sticking and twisting in his gut. He'd run this conversation over and over before it happened, but all his preparation was for nothing. The depth of his grief and despair lay open.

He'd lost the love of his life. The one woman who'd understood him. The woman who could help him make sense of all the madness in the world. She'd filled in all the empty spaces. Now that beautiful woman was gone. He hated that the only picture he could remember of her was the final moment in the blood-soaked alley. No one should die in a place like that. Especially his wonderful Jess. *I'm so sorry, Jess.*

To his surprise, Jess's father was still on the line when he picked it up.

"Son, are you OK?"

*How can he ask me something like that right now? Shouldn't he be yelling and screaming at the man that got his daughter killed?*

"Yeah, I'm OK. Frank, I just want to say I'm sorry..."

"It wasn't your fault, son. You did your best. Jess wouldn't want you to blame yourself."

Cal could barely keep his voice above a whisper. "I know."

"When can we come see you?"

"I'd really rather come to you guys," Cal said. "When's Jess's funeral?"

"We were waiting to hear from you. When are they releasing you?"

"I'm not sure. I've got a couple other phone calls to make. Can I call you back when I know more?"

"Sure." Frank paused for a beat. "And, Cal?"

"Yeah."

"I love you, son."

Unable to respond, the tear-soaked Marine hung up the call. He couldn't bring himself to turn his head and see the picture of his beloved, captured in one of their happiest moments. He understood now why some cultures erase all physical traces of a deceased family member. We are finite vessels, after all, and some grief is just too much to bear. He realized that not even a lifetime in battle could prepare you for the death of a loved one. The pit of emptiness he felt in his stomach threatened to overwhelm him. He tried to push it away.

*Work, dammit. I have to work.*

He took a cleansing breath, followed it with a healthy swig of tepid hospital coffee, and turned to the stack of hand-written phone messages.

The next calls were from his cousin, Travis Haden, a former Navy SEAL who ran Cal's father's company.

He speed-dialed Travis and waited for his cousin to answer.

"Cal?"

Cal took a deep breath before answering. "Hey, Trav."

"Shit, man." Cal could hear the relief in his voice. "What the hell is going on? Why didn't you return my calls? Me and some of the boys were about to raid the hospital!"

"I've had a lot on my mind, Trav."

Trav's voice grew softer. "Yeah, I know. I can't tell you how sorry I am about Jess, cuz."

"Thanks, but I really don't wanna talk about it."

"OK. How about you? How are you feeling?"

"It's never fun to be shot, but I'm doing OK."

"What are the doctors saying?"

"They say I need some physical therapy and want me to stay here for a couple weeks. Is there anything you can do about that?"

Travis always seemed to know someone that could pull a few strings. "I've already looked into it. How about we get you a ride in an ambulance back to the compound and have a doctor check on you a couple times a day?"

Cal thought about the two-thousand-acre campus south of Nashville that housed Stokes Security International (SSI). It would be good to see it again. "I'd love it. I can even put up with any doctor if I can come home."

"You got it, Cal. Let me make some calls. You sit tight and I'll call you back within the hour."

With that, the phone went dead and Cal put it back on the nightstand.

The rest of the messages were from friends/employees within SSI. He'd wait until he got back to the compound before talking to them.

True to his word, Travis called back within the hour.

"So, I talked to the hospital staff and they weren't too happy about the situation, but I explained that we'd have a doc to escort you back to the compound and that he'd be on-call twenty-four-seven."

Relief flooded Cal's body. "Cool. Thanks for doing that."

"They only had one request. I guess they've got some male nurse taking care of you?"

"Yeah. Former corpsman. Good guy."

"Perfect. Can you get him on the phone?"

"Yeah, hang on while I press the call button."

Thirty seconds later, Brian walked into the room. "What's up, Marine?"

"I need you to do me a favor. My cousin's on the phone and he's helping me get out of here. He needs to talk to you about some request the hospital's made."

Brian tilted in head in confusion but nodded and grabbed the phone. "This is Brian Ramirez."

Cal watched as Brian nodded his head and grunted "yes" a couple times. Then he said, "Yeah, I can take some time off."

Cal couldn't hear the conversation but he had a feeling about what was coming.

"OK," Brian said. "I'll see you soon."

Brian handed the phone back to Cal.

"You wanna tell me what's going on, Trav?" Cal asked.

"Brian will fill you in on the details. We're working to get the ball rolling and get you out of there today."

"Awesome. Thanks again."

"No worries. I'll see you soon."

Cal replaced the phone on the nightstand and looked at Brian. "What was that all about?"

"Your cousin just hired me for a couple weeks."

"*He what?!*"

"I guess the hospital would only let you out of here if one of their staff went along with you," Brian explained. "Since I've been your wet nurse they figured I was a perfect fit. That way the hospital minimizes its legal exposure and you get good care. I've got some time off I can take anyway AND your cousin said he'd put me up in that compound place and pay me double what I make here. Any chicks in the compound?"

Cal laughed. "Only one and you don't want to mess with her."

"OK, then let me get some things together and I'll pack up your stuff. Anything you need?"

"Any way I can avoid you being my babysitter?"

"Not if you want get out of this hospital. Just suck it up, Marine, and let me get paid."

Cal reclined again and turned his eyes back up to the ceiling. It wouldn't be so bad having Brian around. Walking was still a chore. Having someone he knew pushing him around in a wheelchair might be OK. Plus, the compound was a big place and he'd have way more to do there than he would sitting around the hospital. Hell, SSI was technically *his* company after all.

The future brimmed with possibilities.

Chucking pencils at the ceiling wasn't one of them.

## CAMP SPARTAN, ARRINGTON, TN

"OK, Cal, we're pulling into the compound. How are you feeling?"

The voice belonged to Dr. Rich Hadley, the physician Travis had hired.

"I'm good," Cal said, coming to after a quick doze in the ambulance. "Here already? I was just getting used to your stories."

Dr. Hadley chuckled. He did not have what you would call a 'normal' medical practice. After successfully completing his double residency and fellowship in internal medicine and general surgery, Dr. Hadley had decided to take a left turn, becoming a concierge doctor for the country music stars in the Nashville area. It was "Music City" after all.

It was a great conversation starter, which had paved the way for a sort of interview session Cal conducted to pass the time on the car ride.

Dr. Hadley had struggled for the first couple years after school, until he'd met Cal's cousin Travis. Travis, being the social butterfly that he was, quickly became friends with outgoing and adventurous Dr. Hadley. Both were in their late thirties and had the luck of being endowed with rugged good looks. Both shared of love of two things: outdoors and women.

Between the pair, they'd cut a wide swath within the ranks of the southern belles in Nashville.

Over time, Travis had introduced Dr. Hadley to his country music friends. In the past five years his private concierge practice had grown to include most of the respected country singer/songwriters in the area. Why go to a crowded clinic when you can call your own doctor?

Dr. Hadley had also been more than happy to help Travis and SSI on occasion. This was one of those times.

"Once we stop I'll have some of the guys lower your stretcher down and roll you into the VIP quarters."

"Travis is putting me in VIP?" Cal asked.

"You'd rather he put you in one of the Quonset huts?"

"Not really."

"Good. Now make sure you don't move around while they cart you in. Travis would be pissed if I delivered his favorite cousin in a bloody mess."

"Whatever you say, doc."

The ambulance pulled to a stop and Cal could hear the driver getting out of the cab and closing the door. The back doors were opened and Cal saw a couple of the roving security guards moving in to help lift the gurney out of the ambulance.

Cal looked around and felt the pull of home. He'd spent plenty of time in the compound that his father had christened "Camp Spartan" due to his fascination with the ancient warriors of Sparta, but also due to the fact that it was a fairly accurate description of the spartan facilities.

Much of the compound was modeled after Marine Corps bases. You had headquarters and then separate buildings for each division. Battalions were located on the lower levels of their respective division.

Cal's father had put a lot of time into hiring former military. He understood that these warriors craved the familiar look and feel of military surroundings. That's not to say that the grounds weren't state of the art. Cal Sr. had insisted on having a top-notch facility while at the same time maintaining a Marine Corps look and feel.

The compound was actually more of a campus. The mess hall was located behind the headquarters building, and the living quarters just behind that. One of the things the company found was that many of the families of employees also enjoyed living in close proximity, just as they had on military bases around the world. As a result, a portion of the campus was devoted to single-family homes for the families of SSI employees. There was even a condominium compound for non-married employees.

It was easy for spouses to come home for lunch or meet their families to eat in the mess hall. Needless to say, morale was high as was retention within SSI.

The exception to the spartan décor was the VIP quarters. Housed on the highest point of the property, the structure looked like a huge hunting lodge resplendent with a carved log exterior and large paneled windows. There were even rocking chairs on the huge front deck for visitors to enjoy.

The entire structure stood at right around 30,000 square feet with ten large guest suites. It was, therefore, no wonder that the employees had taken to calling it the Lodge.

Soon after SSI experienced its enormous growth, Cal Sr. realized the benefit of having the ability to house VIPs on site. It allowed visitors to see firsthand the inner workings of Stokes Security International. If potential clients weren't sold after the initial presentation, they certainly were after being wined and dined by the staff at the Lodge.

Dr. Hadley directed the paramedics to take Cal up through the ramped entrance. Cal noticed Brian standing next to his car parked in front. The former corpsman walked over and followed the crew into the building.

Brian leaned over and whispered in Cal's ear. "Do I get to stay in here too?"

They moved into the inner sanctum of the Lodge. An old-fashioned bar, fully stocked, stood in the corner facing a variety of comfortable looking leather chairs.

"I'm sure they're gonna put you in one of the suites next to where they've got me."

"Suite?"

"Yeah." Cal laughed. "They've each got a couple bedrooms and a nice living area. This is where the company houses visitors, prospective employees and VIPs."

Brian continued to stare wide-eyed as they passed through each enormous room. "Are they looking to have an old corpsman turned nurse on staff?"

"I don't know. I'll ask."

Cal smiled at his friend, glad to have some levity in an otherwise degrading experience of being wheeled in on a gurney.

They arrived at a bank of elevators. Dr. Hadley pressed the button for the second floor. "Travis has you in the corner suite."

Cal nodded. He thought that's where they'd keep him. The corner suite was more like a Presidential Penthouse. 4,000 square feet of living area, way more than he needed, but at least he could take advantage of the view. The floor to ceiling windows overlooked the majority of Camp Spartan. It would be good to see it again.

The team moved into the oversized elevator and it rose to the second level. Exiting the elevator, they turned to the right and headed to the end of the hall. One of the staff members withdrew a card key, inserted it in the lock and held the door open for the stretcher.

Brian, who'd been following behind, let out a small, impressed gasp.

The place was huge. Furnished with the same décor as the rest of the Lodge.

"What do you think?" Cal called back to him.

"I think the corner suite is bigger than any house I've ever lived in."

Dr. Hadley was all business as he instructed the crew to move Cal to the oversized sofa that faced the glassed wall. With some effort Cal scooted to the edge of the gurney, maneuvered over to the sofa, and sat back.

"I'll call Travis and let him know you're settled," said Dr. Hadley. "I'm sure he already knows you're here, but he wanted me to give him a heads-up once you were safely in your room."

"Great. Now I'm gonna have to check in with Trav before I take a piss."

Dr. Hadley pursed his lips. "You know he's only looking out for you, Cal."

"I know, Doc."

"Here's my card. If you need anything call me. For the rest, Brian will take care of you. I'll stop by a couple times a day to check in. I'm right down the hall."

"You're staying here too?"

Dr. Hadley grinned. "Are you kidding? Have you had the bread pudding here? If your cousin is going to employ me I will be happy to take full advantage. Besides, my place is thirty minutes away and Travis' instructions were for me to be immediately available."

"Thanks for doing that, Doc."

"Don't thank me. Thank Travis for paying my enormous bill."

The good-looking doctor smiled and left the room.

Cal turned to Brian. "I'll bet he's not even charging us. The good doctor tries to play the part of the money-hungry surgeon but it's obvious he enjoys this cloak and dagger stuff."

"Yeah, I got the same vibe. Seems like a pretty good guy. You know, for a doctor."

"Yeah."

"All right. So now you're gonna tell me what the hell this place is. What does your dad's company do? They must be making millions."

Cal laughed. "You want the long or the short version?"

"Where do I have to go? I'm your babysitter, remember?"

"Don't remind me. OK, I'll start at the beginning..."

# CALVIN STOKES SR.

C al's father was a rising star in the Marine Corps during the first Gulf War in the early nineties. He'd been commissioned in 1971 just as the Vietnam War was in full swing. After attending The Basic School, he'd been shipped first to Okinawa, Japan, and then to Vietnam.

He'd commanded a platoon and earned a Purple Heart and a Silver Star during his two tours. Cal remembered how his father had described those times patrolling the paddies and jungles of Vietnam. It was also where he'd learned the importance of two things: completing the mission and taking care of your Marines. It was a lesson he carried on in all aspects of his life up until the day he died.

Throughout the seventies and eighties, Cal Sr. moved up through the ranks while at the same time moving his small family all over the world. There were stints in Camp Pendleton, Monterey, Okinawa, Camp Lejeune, Nashville for recruiting duty, and more. Along the way he and Cal's mother, Denise, bore a healthy and rambunctious little boy.

Cal had enjoyed his early days on Marine Corps bases. Living on a military base had its perks: a high level of security for family, a large number of young children to play with, good prices for food and a solid school system. It was a life you could get used to.

Needless to say, over the years Cal Sr. did more deploying than fathering. That wasn't to say that he was a bad father. Actually, the opposite was the case. He cherished his time at home with his wife and son and took full advantage of being on leave.

As Cal closed in on his teenage years, tensions increased in the Middle East culminating in Iraq's invasion of neighboring Kuwait. He remembered watching the footage with his mother, both knowing that it was only a matter of time before Col. Stokes would lead his Marines into battle.

Sure enough, orders were quickly passed down through the ranks and Cal Sr. headed to war commanding his regiment of Marines.

Left at home, Cal's behavior took a nose dive. In retrospect, Cal understood that the way he'd acted was his method of dealing with the possibility that his father could die. First it was talking back in school. Then it was a fight with one of his classmates. Finally, Cal was arrested by the Camp Lejeune military police when he got caught breaking into the PX at two in the morning trying to steal cigarettes.

Cal's mother was devastated. Not only was her husband at war, her only son was now a criminal.

Word travels fast on Marine bases and this was no exception. Mrs. Stokes soon received a request by the base commanding general to come for lunch. The wives of Marine colonels do not get invited to lunch with generals. If anything, it would have been the general's wife doing the inviting.

Again, not so in this case. Mrs. Stokes arrived at the commanding general's quarters the next day. She was ushered in by the general's aide.

General Willard met her at the entrance to the dining room. "Nice to see you again, Denise."

"Thank you for having me," she said demurely.

"Why don't we have a seat. Gunny Fred is about to bring out some club sandwiches. Does that sound OK?"

"That would be fine."

The two moved to the dining room table. The leaves had all been taken out and what could at times seat twenty officers and wives now could only seat six diners total.

They both sat down and the food followed shortly. The general made small talk as they ate. Ten minutes later they were both finished and Gen. Willard began.

"Denise, I just wanted to have you by so I could make sure everything's going OK at home. I know how trying it is to have Colonel Stokes overseas. Add to that the mischief Cal Jr's been getting in and I know you have your hands full."

More than anything at that minute Denise Stokes, a proud southern woman and wife of a Marine colonel, was embarrassed and frightened. She'd always enjoyed the evenings at the Officer's Club mingling with the other wives. This was something entirely different. To be summoned to the throne room was unbearable.

"General, I know there's nothing that can fix what my son has done. I only ask that he be given the punishment he deserves and maybe he'll learn his lesson. I will say that I have tried my best but sometimes teenage boys don't want to listen to their mothers."

"I appreciate you saying that, Denise," said General Willard. "You do, however, realize that Cal Jr. is part of the Marine family and as a Marine I have a duty to help."

"I understand."

"How about I have a little talk with the boy? Maybe even give him a tour of the local juvenile detention facility. I know the warden pretty well and he's always happy to help me keep our kids on the straight and narrow."

"If you think that would help, I'd be much obliged."

General Willard nodded sharply. "Consider it done." He turned to the door and yelled for his aide. "Captain Nelson!"

Capt. Nelson walked into the room. "Yes, General?"

"Please schedule to have my driver pick up young Calvin from the Stokes residence tomorrow morning at 06:00. Bring him to the PT field and then I'll ride back with him to the office."

"Yes, sir."

General Willard turned back to Mrs. Stokes. "Well then, Denise, please don't hesitate to call if you need anything. Anything at all."

"Thank you, Sir."

She sincerely hoped she would never have to call the General. She picked up her pocketbook and made her way to the door.

The next morning, right at 06:00, Calvin Stokes Jr. was waiting with his mother on the front step of their two-story home. He wore his best Sunday khaki slacks with a white button-down shirt. His hair was buzz cut as he'd worn it during the past year and the look of anger and dejection was evident on his face.

The night before when his mother had arrived at home, she'd delivered the news. A screaming match ensued ending with Cal slamming his bedroom door in her face. Temper tantrum or not, he was ready for the General's driver at 05:30. He knew the alternative.

Without an appetite, he waited quietly, glaring at his mother as she'd casually eaten her own breakfast.

A government vehicle pulled up at 06:00 and what looked to be a six-foot five Marine sergeant stepped out of the driver's seat. He was dressed in firmly creased utilities and marched smartly to the door.

The sergeant had a baritone voice. "Mrs. Stokes?"

"Yes, Sergeant, I'm Mrs. Stokes."

"Is the young Mr. Stokes ready to go?"

"He sure is, Sergeant. I appreciate you coming out here to get him."

"Not at all, ma' am. You ready to go son?"

Cal sounded nervous when he answered. "Yes, Sir."

"Don't call me Sir, son. You can call me Sergeant Kraus."

"Yes, Sergeant Kraus."

"Well let's get going. The General's waiting."

He walked back to the car and held the back door open for Cal. Cal slid into the back seat and fastened his seat belt. Sgt. Kraus waved goodbye to Cal's mother and walked around the car into the driver's seat.

Kraus started the car and they began their trek. Cal looked back to see his mother still standing on front step. Too mad and embarrassed to move, he didn't even wave back.

The next eight hours were torture for Cal. Sgt. Kraus picked up the general at the PT field and then took the pair back to the Headquarters building. The whole way not a word was spoken to Cal who sat sullen in the back. All his bluster from the night before had evaporated.

After a stern talking to while standing at attention in front of the general's huge desk, he was taken by the ever-present Sgt. Kraus to the juvenile detention facility just off base in Jacksonville, NC.

There the warden, stone-faced but cordial, instructed his staff to get Cal dressed in a prison jumpsuit. He'd changed into the oversized outfit under the disapproving glare of two male and one female guard.

Then the warden, followed closely by Sgt. Kraus and the

three prison guards, gave Cal a careful tour of the entire facility.

Cal saw the looks on the faces of the kids serving time. Some looked scared. Some looked resigned. Others just looked like career criminals. By the end of the two-hour tour, Cal knew he never wanted to return.

Although the shock of the prison tour seemed effective for the short term, Cal soon fell into his old routines. This go-around, however, he did a better job covering his tracks. He no longer committed outright mischief; instead he skirted the rules and bent them to his will.

Even at a young age, Cal excelled in academics. He'd enjoyed a challenge and far outpaced his classmates. He now used his mind to mold the rules as he saw fit. He was never again caught for any overt acts of fighting or stealing, but he would return home with smoke and beer on his breath. His mother could never prove it.

His behavior remained poor until Cal's father returned from war. The homecoming was more of a relief to Mrs. Stokes than to Cal. He waited with a mixture of fear and anger as his parents discussed his fate.

Looking back, Cal knew his disruptive attitude was a kid's way of coping with an absent father, but even in the midst of the turmoil, deep down he knew he'd crossed the line. That did not, however, mean he would beg for forgiveness. It wasn't HIS fault that his father had gone off to war.

Col. Stokes received the news with a strange calm. He'd already been tipped off by a friend on the Commanding General's staff so he knew the majority of Cal's infractions. Coming home from his second war, Cal Sr. understood the actions of young men. When given the chance, they could excel beyond anyone's imagination. Left alone without proper guidance, young boys could just as easily fall on the wrong side of the tracks.

Col. Stokes understood why Cal had misbehaved. It didn't make it right, but it was what it was. So, although his star shined bright within the Marine Corps, Col. Stokes personally delivered his retirement papers to the commander of Second Marine Division the next day. The general did his best to set Cal Sr. against his chosen path, but the Marine and more importantly, the father would not be dissuaded.

Col. Stokes knew it was time to spend more time with his family.

———

THE STOKES FAMILY packed up and relocated back to Nashville, Tennessee, a few weeks later. Through teary goodbyes with lifelong friends and an emotional change of command ceremony where Col. Stokes was awarded the Legion of Merit and a Bronze Star, the Stokes clan moved on, uncertain of the future.

Cal Sr. used his considerable accrued leave time to reach out to his numerous contacts in the civilian world. Throughout his time in the Corps, he'd come in contact with various influential individuals both on the national and local scene. Although his skills from the Marine Corps didn't equate to one particular job in the civilian world (not many regiments to command on Main Street U.S.A.), his Marine determination knew he would find something.

He spent his days making phone calls and his nights and weekends with the family. Most time devoted to the family found Cal and his father bonding and figuring out each other. There were camping and fishing trips. All the while, Cal's father treated his son like a man and started to relay life's lessons.

Cal's spirits and attitude improved. He'd needed his father and once again things felt right in the world.

Not long after settling in the Nashville suburb of Franklin, TN, Cal Sr. was hired by a local government facility as a consultant to evaluate the facility's security and operations. The contact had been arranged by an old friend now serving at the Pentagon who had sung Cal Sr.'s praises to regional director in charge of all of Tennessee state's federal facilities.

Although he'd never done anything like what he'd been hired for, the money was right and like a true Marine, he'd figure it out as he went.

Long story short, after evaluating the facility, interviewing employees, cataloging procedures, and simply observing for six weeks, Col. Stokes delivered his thirty-page summary to the regional director. The director was very pleased with the recommendations and asked Cal Sr. to stay on-board to help implement his suggestions.

Cal's father didn't want to be employed by the government, so instead he asked if a new consulting contract could be drafted for the follow-up work. The director agreed and Cal Sr. spent the good part of the next six months retraining the facility staff and implementing the upgraded security protocol.

During the entire process he made it absolutely clear that the job would not interfere with his home life. He insisted on leaving no later than four thirty each day in order to spend time with Cal. It was a habit that he'd continue until the day he died.

Throughout his first consulting gig, Cal Sr. began to see the possibilities in the world of national and international security. He'd recognized the rise of international terrorist cells during his time in the Marine Corps. He's lost friends in the Beirut bombing. Col. Stokes knew it wouldn't be long before those attacks hit American soil.

Over the next couple years, he formalized the structure of Stokes Security International. He leveraged his abundant contacts within state and federal agencies to help win jobs that included law enforcement training, security analysis, VIP protection, etc. Over time, his staff grew as did his reputation for being absolutely dependable.

He refused jobs that would take him away for long periods of time. He refused offers from certain Middle East governments with reported ties to developing terrorist organizations. While no longer an active duty Marine, Col. Stokes still felt an intense desire to protect and defend the United States.

Along the way, he hired former military officers and enlisted men to be part of the growing SSI. He soon became known within certain circles as the man who gave second chances. Col. Stokes knew from experience that everyone has at least one bad day and sometimes good troops fall by the wayside.

His first "second chance" hire, strangely enough, was Cal's cousin Travis. At the time Travis was a Navy Lieutenant serving as a platoon commander with the SEALs. A highly intelligent young man (Rhodes Scholar in college), and an impressive athlete who'd started at defensive back on Ole Miss football team for four years, Travis seemed to be on the fast track to Navy stardom.

That all changed when he found out that one of his SEALs was beating his wife. A deeply honorable man, Travis confronted the enlisted man. During the short conversation the SEAL admitted to abusing his wife and told Travis it wasn't any of his business.

Although the sailor outweighed Travis by almost fifty pounds, he still found himself waking up inside a San Diego hospital with a broken arm, a dislocated shoulder, a cracked jaw, four broken ribs, a broken leg and one helluva headache.

Travis, after calling the ambulance, turned himself in to the Shore Patrol and was confined at the brig until the unconscious SEAL could wake up and testify against his platoon commander.

The man decided not to press charges but the damage had already been done. By turning himself in, Travis had admitted his guilt. There was nothing the Special Operations community could do except let him leave the Navy quietly. At least it was better than spending more time in the brig.

Cal Sr. found out about the incident from his brother, Travis' father. He invited Travis to fly out to Nashville to spend a little time with family. During the two-week stay, Cal's father introduced Travis to the inner workings of SSI He never made it seem like he was courting a new employee; instead, he quizzed Travis on how SSI could improve its operations.

By the end of the visit, without prompting, Travis made up his mind. He asked his uncle if he could join the company. He explained that he would rather sweep floors for his uncle's company than to beg for work elsewhere.

Needless to say, Cal Sr. took him up on his offer. Instead of starting Travis as he'd requested on the bottom of the totem pole, the CEO of SSI took Travis under his wing. For the first year he rarely left Cal Sr.'s side. Some people called Travis "The Bodyguard" but he served as more of an aide and apprentice. Travis would later admit that the time spent with his uncle and his family probably saved him from a depressive fate.

Never a word was said by the rest of the company staff other than to give the new man a friendly ribbing. Many within SSI came from similar backgrounds and circumstances. It was the former Marine turned CEO who had helped many of his staff over the years. They respected their leader's decisions and believed in his vision.

The second and probably more important reason, was that the entire company harbored a deep and open respect for the Stokes family. Col. Stokes was a tough man but a fair man. He always made time for his family and was known for walking the halls and kicking his employees out so they could spend time with their own loved ones.

Every person up and down the chain felt like they had earned the title of SSI employee. The feeling was very similar to the young man crossing the parade deck and finally being called a Marine. It was an atmosphere that Cal Sr. worked hard to foster from the beginning.

Other key players in the SSI family also came from employment similar to Cal's cousin. There was the logistics chief, Martin Farmer, a former Marine Master Sergeant who'd been relieved of duty after falling deep into alcoholism and depression upon coming home from deployment to find his wife sleeping with the Marine next door. There had been no violence, only the swift decline of a man once revered by his peers and now hindered by the bottle.

Farmer's crusty old Sergeant Major was the one to give Col. Stokes the heads-up. The Sergeant Major and Colonel had served together on two separate occasions and held each other in high regard. So, when the phone call came from his former Marine, he was glad to help.

He'd reviewed the Master Sergeant's record that, minus the present problem, was exemplary including two meritorious promotions. Next, he hopped a flight to Camp Lejeune and was formally introduced by the Sergeant Major.

Col. Stokes recognized the pain in the man's eyes and made a deal with him. He would pay for the man's rehabilitation and counseling. At the end of the program if Farmer came out clean, he would be hired at SSI. Like most Marines, MSgt Farmer was a proud man and fully appreciated the helping hand he'd received. He flew through recovery and reported in to work ninety days later, right after a brief stop in North Carolina to finalize his divorce.

MSgt Farmer became one of Cal Sr.'s brightest stars and totally revamped SSI's logistics division. It seemed early on that Col. Stokes had an eye for talent.

All along the way, Cal Jr. became a welcome aide to the SSI CEO. He'd often sit in on high level meetings and interviews. Sometimes he was in the room; other times he was next door listening through the conference intercom system. Cal learned that his father was a special man that invested in his fellow man first in order to better himself and others. Cal learned that his father had a special place in his heart for those in need of a second chance, but that second chances always came with stipulations. Cal Sr.'s sense of morality was strong when it came down to the activity that caused any potential employee to get into trouble.

He remembered the time an old friend had gone out on a limb for a certain Navy Master Chief. Apparently the two didn't quite know each other but somehow the Master Chief knew enough people to get referred to Col. Stokes. The story Cal Sr. received from his old friend differed drastically from the story that finally came out of the ill-fated Master Chief's mouth. Apparently, the sailor believed that *any* first infraction warranted a second chance in the mind of the founder of SSI. He soon found out otherwise.

It quickly surfaced that the man had twisted his story in order to gain sympathy with his former commander. The commander, an old friend of Col. Stokes, took the man for his word and was more than happy to pass along a supposedly trust-worthy sailor to his buddy.

It turned out that the man had severely beaten two young sailors who'd just reported into his unit. Apparently, alcohol was involved, and what started as an innocent hazing ritual soon turned violent.

Sitting in front of Col. Stokes, it was obvious the sailor still held no remorse for the situation. He actually had the audacity to blame the Navy for accusing him unjustly. Little did the man know that Col. Stokes held no room in his world for bullies and liars. The man was swiftly escorted out by Travis and two other former SEALs, and a report was submitted to Col. Stokes' friend which he in turn filed with the Navy.

It was during this altercation that Cal finally understood his father's true sense of right and wrong. He believed that any abuse or offense against a lesser human being was morally wrong. At the same time, Cal Sr. did believe that there are times when a man must take the law into his own hands as long as it was the right thing to do.

Cal asked his father about this supposed duplicity and he'd listened as Cal Sr. calmly explained that although America was the best country in the world, even America's laws were not always fair to all and oftentimes sheltered criminals for the sake of due process.

His son knew his father approved certain covert missions for various government agencies that, if seen by the liberal media, would be criticized as being barbaric and unconstitutional. Each of these undertakings was always scrutinized for its ethical basis by the headquarters team at SSI. A mission was never green-lighted if the outcome and the methods did not live up to SSI's high moral standard.

Col. Stokes would later solidify his belief with a motto he would dub Corps Justice.

## CAMP SPARTAN, ARRINGTON, TN

"So, let me get this right," Brian said. "This company is gonna be yours?"

"Well, I guess technically it is mine," Cal admitted.

"Holy shit! You're like a billionaire!"

Cal felt sheepish. "Not really. I guess you'd call me a multi-millionaire. Don't spread that around."

"Are you kidding me?! No one would believe that a dumb grunt like you is a billionaire anyway."

"Millionaire!"

Brian waved him off. "Whatever. It's all the same."

"Do you even know the difference? Anyway, do you want to hear the rest of the story of not?"

"All right, go on Mr. Billionaire."

Cal ignored the comment and continued. "So, my Dad taught me that many worlds exist within the law. He learned early on in the security business that he would have access to certain intel that could benefit others for good and bad. His deep sense of moral duty kept him from profiting from the bad side. At the same time, he knew there was a huge gray area left for him to interpret."

"I'm not following you."

"OK." Cal took a deep breath before continuing. "I remember Dad telling me the story of the first instance when he hit a real gray area. On a certain job a few years back, one of his SSI passive surveillance teams found out that a neighbor of the target was running an illegal prostitution and drug ring and that both the woman and drugs were being supplied from Taiwan."

"All right. So, he just gave that intel to the cops, right?"

Cal shook his head. "Nope. Think about it. Every American citizen has a certain right to privacy. Technically, the intel was gathered because one of the team members was curious about the girls coming in and out of the house. So, the team shifted a couple of listening devices over to the other house along with a camera and just monitored it for a couple days. Well, they found out pretty quickly what was going on but the dilemma was the legality of the source of information. Any two-bit lawyer could've had the case thrown out of court."

"There's gotta be something the authorities could've done."

"Their hands are tied, man. They would've loved nothing more than to bust that whole thing down. Our company has a lot of contacts in local law enforcement so one of our guys cautiously asked what they would do with the situation without giving away the details like location, etcetera. The cops basically said that unless they were allowed to build the case from the ground up or catch the ring red-handed, there's not much they could do."

"But that's bullshit! They're here to protect us from that kind of stuff."

"I know. But remember that in order to live in a democracy like we have in this country, certain laws must be in place to protect individual freedom and avoid abuse of that freedom."

"Alright, so you're telling me that your dad just sat on the intel and did nothing?"

Cal smiled. "That's the opposite of what he did."

"You gonna tell me or just sit there with that cheesy grin on your face?"

"I know I don't have to say this to you but I will anyways: you can't say anything about what you see around here to anyone outside SSI. Oh, and don't go telling Travis what I've told you. I don't think he'd care, considering who you are, but I don't want him to think I've been running my mouth."

"Who do you think I am? I know how to keep my mouth shut."

"OK. So, my Dad ordered the team to wait until the original mission was over. He didn't want to tip off the ring leaders. Once the first job was finished, the team covertly rounded up all the ringleaders and made them get caught."

"Hold on. What do you mean *made* them get caught?"

"Some of our top snoopers caught the guys, tranquilized them and set them all up in one of their vans in a park down the street." Cal laughed at the memory. "The team loaded the criminals with some booze and their own dope so it looked like they'd passed out after a little partying. They loaded all the drugs and weapon stash in the back of the van so when the cops were anonymously tipped off, the drug dealers and pimps woke up to a slew of cops yelling at them to come out with their hands up and get on the ground. I heard the whole thing was pretty funny."

"What about the slaves they had in the house?"

"For their own safety, they were knocked out too and a minor fire was set. Just enough for the alarm system to alert the fire department. When the fire department busted in and searched the house, they found the girls locked in a back room."

"I still don't see why the cops couldn't have just knocked down the door and swept the place."

"That sounds easy but think about those raids you did with your Marines over in Iraq. Did you ever like going into a situation not knowing what you were gonna get? Who knew what those guys would've done to the local cops busting down the door? The way our team did it, no one was hurt and the criminals were dealt with." Brian still didn't look totally convinced. "Are you really so naïve to think that the police can do anything they want? Come on, doc. You've seen the shitty things people do in this world."

"I know." Brian sounded resigned. "I guess I never really thought about it that much until now. It's like the cops are handcuffed from doing their duty. Reminds me of those times in Iraq when the Rules of Engagement kept my Marines from killing bad guys."

Cal nodded. "Exactly. If they don't do things by the book, these good cops that don't get paid squat could lose their jobs. The law's made it to where police hesitate because they're worried about getting in trouble."

"Yeah. Last week I saw that some cop was getting sued by a guy who got shot while robbing a bank. The cop shot him *after* the guy shot one of the tellers and refused to give up. It's bullshit."

"Yep. That's where Corps Justice comes in."

"Explain that," Brian said.

"Well, like I told you before, my Dad lived and breathed the Marine Corps way. It was my fault he got out of the Corps, but you could never take the Corps out of him. That, mixed with his moral sense of right and wrong, made him adopt his motto about Corps Justice."

"So, is this *Corps Justice* like a company credo or something?"

"Kind of. It's more of an overarching guidance for SSI employees for when they encounter gray areas. Hang on a sec."

Cal grabbed his wallet and pulled out what looked like a business card on tattered paper. He handed it to Brian. "I got that from my Dad when I went off to college."

Brian looked down at the card:

# CAMP SPARTAN, ARRINGTON, TN

**- CORPS JUSTICE -**
**1. We will protect and defend the Constitution of the United States.**
**2. We will protect the weak and punish the wicked.**
**3. When the laws of this nation hinder the completion of these duties, our moral compass will guide us to see the mission through.**

B rian looked up at Cal. "This looks like you can do whatever you want as long as you think it's right."

"I know that's how it seems, but you have to remember that my Dad's moral compass wouldn't allow us to conduct acts of undue aggression. Besides, only the top management within SSI can green light those kinds of jobs. Dad hand-picked that leadership."

"Does this come up a lot?"

Cal shrugged. "I don't think so. Keep in mind that most of the work SSI does is consulting and training. Yes, we do have security teams and quick reaction forces, but most of the missions they undertake are cut and dry. There's typically a clear bad guy and that's who we're sent in to take care of."

"It sounds more like the gigs you take on are government sanctioned."

"Keep in mind that I don't know everything. I don't work here. But you're right. The federal government is our biggest customer, but we have a lot of divisions that trump even that big account."

Brian scratched his chin. "Like what?"

"We do a lot of R&D work and either sell the final product or retain the rights. There's a lot of money in that kind of stuff."

"I'll bet. Are you gonna run the company?"

"Nope. Trav is better at it than I would be. I'll probably be involved somehow but he's a much better schmoozer than I am. Plus, I've still got some things to take care of."

Cal gazed out the expansive windows, trying to stop the intrusion of memory.

"So," said Brian, "tell me how the hell you went into the Marine Corps instead of working here?"

Cal maintained his gaze for a moment, then turned to Brian. "I started my first year of college at the University of Virginia in 1998. My parents were excited about the high caliber of the university, but they still wanted me close. By that time, the company was doing a lot more work with the feds. Dad had anticipated the rise of terrorism and built the company to combat those threats with the ability to augment the American military. He was even doing some work for our allies like the U.K. and Germany."

He paused and shifted his weight trying to find the right words. "Like I said, my parents were really happy about me going to UVA but still wanted to see me. I wanted the same thing. We'd been through a lot together. The great thing about money is that there's not much you can't do when you have it. At that point, SSI was probably a tenth of what it is now but Mom and Dad had more money than they could ever spend. Well, on one of their trips to Charlottesville to watch a UVA football game and visit me, Dad went house shopping. I thought he was just looking for a condo or something they could stay in for weekend trips in. Dad didn't come from much money but always loved the idea of owning land. He always told me that land was one thing you could never reproduce or take away from a man. In Albemarle County, Virginia there's a lot of land. You know Monticello, right?"

"Yeah, that was Thomas Jefferson, right?"

"Yep. Founded UVA too. Anyways, there are a lot of estates like that out there. So, Dad goes out and finds a spread a lot like this one here. Around two thousand acres. He called it his little getaway. What he ended up doing was turning that into our second headquarters. He called it Camp Cavalier because I was at UVA. It turned out great because he built an almost identical campus there that we have here in Nashville. That gave the SSI the ability to be really close to Washington, D.C."

"I'll bet your parents spent more time there too."

"Yeah. It was great to have them close by and they understood that I needed my space too. They'd come over for football games and sometime take me out to dinner. That was a great three years."

Cal paused and returned his gaze to the window and continued. "In the fall of 2001, I was starting my last year in school. My parents had just been by to visit, then headed up to D.C. to visit new clients and old friends. They were going to jump on a plane out to Los Angeles for a quick vacation then head down to Camp Pendleton to see some more friends and fit a little work in too. My parents boarded American Airlines Flight 77 the morning of September 11th. They tried to call me from the flight when it became clear to my Dad that the flight was hijacked. I was in class and didn't get the call. Both calmly told me that they loved me in hushed voices and my Dad told me they'd always be with me."

Tears were now streaming down Cal's face, but he continued. "I could hear my Mom try to choke back her gasps. My Dad was all business, but he still sounded scared. More than anything, I think he was worried for my Mom and for me. That's the way he always was. He finished the message by telling me how proud he was, and that I'd been his greatest accomplishment on earth."

Cal stopped again. His breath now coming in gasps. "I never got to say goodbye. Those fucking terrorist thugs took the most important people out of my life. I sat there playing that message over and over again as I sat with my classmates watching the attacks on TV. I was just numb. Before I knew it, a couple guys from our Charlottesville headquarters barged into the room and found me. Apparently, Travis had sent them to come get me and secure me somewhere."

He reached down and grabbed the bottom of his shirt and wiped his eyes. Then, anger iced his veins. "They tried to take me out of there but I shook them off. One of the guys tried to get me on the phone but I wouldn't do it. I ran out of there and went straight to the ROTC building at Maury Hall. I wasn't part of ROTC, but I knew some of the guys. The MOI was a mustang and had served with Dad. I found him and asked him how I could get into the Corps. He was sympathetic but said it wasn't that easy. There were a lot more hurdles going the officer route. Before he could finish, I bolted. I knew where the Marine recruiter's office was and ran all the way there. There were a bunch of other kids there apparently doing the same thing as me. I pushed my way to the front. No one wanted to mess with the sweat-soaked kid with the tears running down his face. The Gunny sitting at the desk glanced up, annoyed that I'd broken his routine. I asked him how I could get to go overseas the fastest. I told him I wanted to kill the people that had killed my parents. His face changed and he softened up. He stood up and took me to the back of the room where we could talk in private. The Gunny told me that he was getting flooded with similar requests and that he only had one slot left to ship kids to boot camp later that week."

Cal took a deep breath. "I asked him how I could get that one spot. He told me I'd have to compete for it and volunteer to be a grunt. Well, being a pretty smart college kid, I aced the enlistment-screening exam and maxed out the physical fitness test that day. I got the slot and left for boot camp two days later."

Cal looked back at Brian and continued. "I know you're thinking that by the time I got on that bus I regretted my decision. Nope. It was the opposite. Every moment I grieved for my parents, I also felt like I was doing *something*. Hell, even if I wound up cleaning latrines, at least I would've been serving. Enlisting in the Marines was the best thing I could've done. The rest is history."

Brian let the words sink in for a minute. "Holy shit, Cal," he said, his voice softened, "I'm really sorry about your parents. I had no idea."

"Yeah, well, it's not something I advertise. Look, Doc, I don't regret what I did then and I definitely don't regret what I did to those gang bangers. If you're not cool with that, maybe you should leave."

Brian's face became indignant. "Who do you think I am? I'm not some pussy that gets sick over a little bit of blood. I don't give a shit that you killed those guys. They deserved it. I wish you'd finished off the other two." He stopped and took a deep calming breath. "Look, I'm here to help, OK? You've gone through some really shitty situations. I'm more concerned about you mentally than some dead criminal."

"I'm fine. I know how to take care of myself."

"Yeah, right. I know you didn't learn *that* in The Corps. We're brothers, remember? You've gotta be straight with me, man!"

Cal snapped his glare back at Brian. "You want me to tell you that my body aches all day because Jess is dead? You want me to tell you that half the day I wish I'd died with her? You want me to tell you that I want to *kill* those motherfuckers over and over again?"

"Yes, as a matter of cold fact! You can't keep that shit inside, man! You've gotta let it out or it'll eat you alive. You've seen some of those boys that come back from the desert and just clam up. Most turn into drunks or druggies. I don't want that you happen to you!"

Cal stared at Brian. The guy was panting from the exertion.

Then it happened.

It was like a door had been opened. He sure as hell didn't open it himself. In walked Jess.

She looked as she had always looked to him. Beautiful, with her thousand-year-old soul staring out through her eyes. And she did all the little things, like stick her tongue out at him when they met eyes across some crowded room; or purse her lips when she was in deep thought, not realizing he was watching. A wordless gesture here and there; her small yet firm hands stirring milk into tea; the clinking of the spoon and the cup. The rolling of her eyes when he made a dumb joke. Her laugh. Her tears. Her smile.

Her smile.

He laid back and threw his hands to his face and sobbed uncontrollably. The bottled-up pain surfaced in full force. He felt Brian's comforting hand on his shoulder.

Maybe it was like this for five, ten minutes. Maybe it was half the night.

He fell away into deep, dreamless sleep.

Brian expertly checked his friend, making sure Cal was OK. It was time for the Marine to get some well-deserved rest. He stood up and walked across the room, sat down in a leather recliner, and began his vigil.

# PART TWO

# N.O.N. SAFE HOUSE, NASHVILLE, TN

"What do you mean he *left?*"

Dante listened to his cell phone as anger raged on his face. "You told me they had to tell you if they were gonna release him. *Fuck.* Did you at least find out where they took him?"

The answer he got was not what he wanted.

"Well then, I guess you're about to have a bad night. And don't even think about not showing up. You've got some explaining to do."

He shut off the call and sat back on the dirty couch. Dante was sick and tired of being on the run. The only good news was that he'd somehow managed to recruit a couple more boys to join his crew. He only got that done by offering way more of cut than he usually did. It really was his only choice. Everyone knew Dante couldn't show his face on the streets.

*Once this thing blows over, I'll take my money back anyway.*

Dante's plan of taking out the hero Marine as he was leaving the hospital was now scrapped. He'd have to find another way to get to the guy. The gang leader was still confused about how the dude had managed to be released without having to go through normal hospital protocol. Maybe there was more to this guy than he knew. He'd have to do some digging.

As he sat thinking in the dingy hideout, a plan began to formulate. If he couldn't get to the Marine himself, he'd somehow have to get him out in the open.

*Think, Dante, think.*

## CAMP SPARTAN, ARRINGTON, TN

Cal awoke to the thin stream of light coming from the curtain-covered bay windows. His eyes focused on Brian asleep in the leather chair across the room. *I'll bet he's been sitting there all night.*

He tested his balance as he slowly rose into a sitting position. His wounds still throbbed but they'd be muted a bit after a couple pain killers. Cal quietly shuffled to the bathroom to relieve himself. After he was done, he brushed his teeth, washed his face, and threw down two pain pills. *Time for breakfast.*

As he walked back into the main room, Brian got up from his chair and did a quick stretch while yawning. "How you feeling, Cal?"

"All right. Listen, about my bawlin' last night, I—"

"Don't worry about it. I'm glad you got it out. Now we can work on getting you better."

Cal nodded, allowing himself this tiny bit of humility. "So, what's on the schedule for today's torture?"

Brian chuckled. "Travis stopped by while you were passed out and he said you guys have a nice gym on campus."

"That we do."

"I thought I'd wheel you over there and we could do some stretches and PT. You up for it?"

"Yeah. I need some fresh air."

"Me too. Let me go take a leak and then I'll help you get changed. You wanna eat before or after?"

"Let's do after. I don't want to puke up everything at the gym. My gut's still not right."

"Cool. Give me a minute and we'll head out."

Fifteen minutes later, the pair emerged from the suite. Cal rested comfortably in an off-road looking wheelchair. *Probably some super upgrade Trav hooked up for me.* At least they could take it on some of the trails if they wanted.

After leaving the Lodge, Cal directed Brian to take a left and head down three blocks. As they traveled Cal described some of the surrounding buildings. "That one over there is the mess hall and the one behind that is the HQ."

At a brisk pace, they reached the gym in only a couple minutes. Although sparsely decorated, it looked to Brian like all the newest equipment was housed within the facility.

"This is the main area with free weights and machines," Cal said. "We've got a cardio room around the corner that has flat screens. Where should we start?"

Brian looked around. "Let's head over to that spot with the mats. We'll kill some stretches first."

Thirty minutes later, Cal was drenched in sweat and panting with exertion. The stretching alone had been excruciating for the wounded warrior. Moving on to the treadmill felt like death. Nevertheless, he finished the tortuous physical therapy session with a determined smile on his face. It felt good to move again.

Brian stood up and surveyed his patient. "All right, that's good for today, Cal."

Cal nodded and rolled over. "Let's go get some food and then I want to introduce you to some people."

Brian looked at his friend quizzically but kept his mouth shut and helped Cal into the wheelchair.

The duo left the gym facility and headed toward the chow hall. As they entered the smell of scrambled eggs and pancakes greeted them. They found a booth in a corner and Cal took a seat.

"What do you want me get for you?" Brian asked.

"Two eggs over-easy, country ham, a stack of pancakes and some orange juice."

"Got it. I'll be right back."

The companions finished breakfast with the occasional greeting from company employees who stopped by to say hello to Cal. Brian noticed that rather than be embarrassed or standoffish, Cal spoke openly with the visitors and knew most by their first names. It wasn't something he'd expected and mentioned this on the way out of the dining facility.

"Yeah, I've spent a lot of time on both campuses over the years," Cal explained. "I've even been in on some of the hiring interviews. Dad really wanted me to see the inner workings at SSI and included me whenever he could. I even had a hand in hiring some employees. That reminds me, take a left up here. I want to introduce you to somebody."

Brian took the next left. They walked down four blocks, finally reaching a low structure. Brian pointed at the front door and Cal nodded. As they passed through the double doors, the former corpsman noticed the pressurized feel as the heavy glass door sucked back into place.

"What is this place?" Brian asked.

"We call it the Bat Cave."

"Guess that makes you Batman," said Brian.

The two strolled up to the front desk. The two security guards, heavily armed, greeted Cal by his first name, coming around the desk to shake his hand. It was obvious to Brian that both men − each the size of an NFL linebacker − liked and respected Cal. These weren't some employees attempting to suck up to the future boss. These guys really admired Cal, and it seemed that they held him on some sort of pedestal. *Interesting*.

They waved goodbye, Cal promising to meet the two guards at the gym soon and headed to the bank of elevators.

They boarded the first to arrive and Brian shifted around to select a floor. There was only a second floor and nine buttons below the first floor. *A bunch of subfloors*. He looked at Cal questioningly.

"Press B9," Cal said.

Brian pressed the very bottom button. *Nine levels down?*

It took less than a minute for the elevator to descend and open its doors. As they opened, Brian smelled the incoming air. It smelled like the air wing hangers he remembered from his time with the Marines. That unique smell of oil, grease and metal. The smell brought back a flood of memories from his time spent at Cherry Point and his cruises on the gator freighters.

Cal took a deep breath. "OK, before we head down to see Neil, I want to give you a little background. Neil was one of my finds for the company. We went to school together at UVA. He was two years ahead of me. He'd been my resident advisor my first year. Neil was a brilliant triple major who hardly studied. He was a funny mix of hip social butterfly and technological genius. I won't tell you what his IQ is, because you won't believe me. So anyways, his family came over from India when Neil was a little kid. They didn't have a lot of money and really worked hard to make ends meet. Fortunately, his father was almost as smart as he is. Mr. Patel started a cell phone company out of his garage, if you can believe it. He grew it into this booming business that he exported back to India. Made a helluva lot of cash. Neil grew up tinkering with the surplus cell phones his dad had lying around. Pretty soon he was doing all the repairs for the company. He just had this knack for fixing and building stuff. There was this little joke around town that he could fix phones by looking at them."

"How'd he wind up in a dump like this?" Brian joked.

Cal smiled. "Well, going into his fifth year at school his mom and dad went on a trip to India then over to Pakistan. Business trip. They were there to meet with contacts who were going to open a new headquarters for Mr. Patel's company. While they were in Pakistan, both of Neil's parents were kidnapped and later killed."

Brian shook his head. "Holy crap."

"Some tiny terrorist outfit claimed responsibility. No one was ever caught."

"I can't imagine how the son must've taken that," Brian said.

"Neil went into a real tailspin. He and his father were really close and Neil didn't know how to cope. He went off the deep end; started drinking all the time, screwing anyone he could get his hands on, and started dabbling in drugs. Let's just say he really didn't give a shit anymore."

Cal looked up at the ceiling. "So I bump into him one night at some party and I notice he's a little crazier than I remember. I somehow convince him to stick around and hang out with me. Over way too many drinks, he finally broke down and told me the story about his parents. Up to that point I'd had no idea. It was obvious that he'd given up and didn't want to deal with life let alone school. Then the poor dude passed out on my couch."

"What'd you do?"

"At the time I didn't know exactly what to do but I knew I had to help the guy. We were little more than casual

acquaintances but he'd always been a great friend. I called my
Dad the next morning and explained the situation. Luckily
Dad was at the Charlottesville headquarters and asked that I
set up a meeting with Neil. I agreed and somehow got a very
hungover Neil into my car and out to Camp Cavalier."

Cal chuckled. "The coffee on the way seemed to revive
him a bit, but pulling into the main gate really woke him up.
Long story short, my Dad instantly liked him and outlined his
plan for Neil. He wanted Neil to lay off the partying and
finish up school. Then he'd bring him on in the company's
brand new R&D department. I think this might've done the
trick, but Dad threw in a kicker. He promised Neil that if he
came onboard, SSI would do anything within its power to
find the men responsible for the Patels' murder and bring
them to justice."

"No shit?"

"Yeah. By that time, Dad had some pretty serious
contacts internationally and within most of our government
agencies. Not to mention SSI's intelligence gathering capabil-
ities were really ramping up. Neil jumped at the chance and
didn't let my Dad down. Six months after Neil graduated, the
terrorist cell that took credit for Neil's parents death were
killed in a raid by Pakistani special forces. Justice was done."

"So, Neil's been here ever since?" Brian asked.

"Yeah. He and my Dad really hit it off. Plus, in no time
Neil was leading the R&D department with some pretty
heavy technological advances. My Dad kept trying to get him
to take a new title like Head of R&D or Vice President for
R&D but Neil always refused. He always said he's just a
developer."

"Developer, huh? What kind of things does he develop?"

"You name it," Cal said. "It started with little tech gadgets
for the military: small cameras, light weaponry, tactical gear.
The guy was a triple engineering major. He'll tell you which

ones but I'll tell you they're all way over my head. Anyways, he and Dad figured out pretty quickly that rather than develop stuff for individual jobs, Neil could instead develop technology that SSI could license out to other entities. Call it the Microsoft model. *That's* when the company really starting making a ton of money. Dad made an agreement with Neil that Neil would keep fifty percent of the sale or ongoing licensing fee from any of the stuff he researched and developed. Neil didn't want the deal, but Dad felt it was only fair. Let's just say that Neil will never have to worry about money ever again."

"So, the guy knows his stuff, huh?"

"He does, but he still tries to play the part of dumb gigolo. I never know how many girlfriends the guy has. Let's go introduce you to Neil."

## NEIL

The men headed straight ahead towards a long corridor lit by fluorescent track lighting. As they neared the room at the opposite end of the hallway, Brian inhaled sharply at the size of the place. It looked like a huge cavern.

"What the hell is this place?"

"I told you, it's the Bat Cave. Head over to the left and that bunch of tables."

At their approach, a slim man in glasses looked up from his work. He stood about six feet tall, slim, like he could've been an actor in Bollywood. Curiously, he wore a pair of black shades around his neck.

Neil took off his reading glasses and walked over to Cal. He bent down to wheelchair level and hugged his friend. "I'm so sorry Cal."

"Thanks."

"Is there anything I can do?"

"We'll get to that in a minute. First, I want you to meet my new friend."

Neil nodded and stood back up. He looked over at Brian

and extended his hand. "Hey, Doc. I'm Neil Patel." He extended both arms. "Welcome to the Bat Cave."

Brian took the man's hand with some trepidation. "Good to meet you, Neil."

Neil smiled conspiratorially and explained. "Don't look so shocked, Doc. Travis sent over your file before you got here. I know all about you."

Brian looked a bit uncomfortable with the lopsided conversation but kept his mouth shut.

Cal stepped in before Neil could make Brian feel even more awkward. "What are you working on?"

Neil gestured grandly to the nearest table and spoke in a mock British accent. "My new toys are waiting for your inspection, good sir."

Cal shook his head and rolled himself over to the table. "What is that? One of those remote-control helicopters from Brookstone?"

Neil made a face of mock indignation and continued in his English accent. "Sir, how dare you accuse me of such a thing! What you see is the latest in nano-drone technology. Courtesy of yours truly." He waved his arms before him and bowed slightly.

Cal picked up the small helicopter-looking device. The thing fit in the palm of his hand and couldn't have been more than the size of a silver dollar in diameter. "Where's the remote?"

Neil pulled off the pair of sunglasses from around his neck. "Right here." He handed the black shades to Cal.

"If this was someone else I'd think they were pulling my leg. But with you I'm pretty sure you're not bullshitting me."

Neil grinned. "Nope. Those sunglasses control the drone. Put 'em on."

Cal did as he was told and put the glasses on. They looked

and felt like a normal pair of sunglasses. "You gonna tell me how this thing works?"

"Push the emblem on the right side of the frame."

Cal did so and immediately the left-hand lens lit up.

It looked like a freaking video game.

He jumped back as the tiny blades on the drone kicked on and set it into a hover. "You could've warned me about that!"

"But then I couldn't have seen the silly look on your face."

"OK. So, what do I do now?"

"You see the screen on the left?" Neil asked.

"Yeah."

"Use your eye and tell the drone where to go."

"Dude. I have no idea what you're talking about."

Neil sounded exasperated, but excited. "Just turn your head and look at something you want the drone to go to."

Cal turned his head and could feel the drone lifting higher. That's when he noticed that the view in the left lens had changed. He was now seeing from the point of view of the drone.

"Holy shit!"

Neil beamed. "I know, right?"

Cal directed the drone to a nearby set of cabinets. He realized that as he focused on an object, the drone would move closer. "How do I keep this thing from running into stuff?"

"You don't. It does. It has a proximity detector. With stationary objects, it's flawless. I'm still working out the kinks on non-stationary objects within the drone's environment. You know, like people running around on the battlefield, cars, animals – anything that moves."

"You can do that?" said Brian, sounding incredulous.

"Pretty easy actually. Hey, Cal., just so you know, the technology in this thing is probably gonna make us all a lot more money. We're thinking we can equip cars with it. Imagine, no more traffic accidents!"

Cal could do nothing but smile with childish bewilderment. This little toy was too much fun. "How do I get it to fly back?"

"Just click that button on the side again and it'll go back to its charging dock over there on that desk."

Cal pressed the button on the sunglasses again. Sure enough, the little drone found its way home, without guidance, to what looked like a miniature landing pad on one of the desks. He removed the shades and handed them back to Neil. "How the hell did you come up with that?"

"Actually, some of the technology's already been around for a while. Apache pilots have been able to control some of their weapons systems with monocles for years. I just made the system better."

"Who are you building it for?" Brian asked.

"No one yet. All the small spy drones right now are way bigger than this little guy. I know there are some other companies in the hunt, but I think ours will be the best. Pretty sure it'll be an easy sell."

"I would've loved one of these over in the desert. Would've made fighting house to house a lot safer if I could send this guy in first."

"That's our target market for this thing," Neil said. "I want to give the troops something that's cost effective and easy to use. A whole freakin' platoon could have one of these things. Trav is talking to a couple of commanders out in the field right now that are gonna try it out for us free of charge."

"You got one that I can borrow?" Cal asked.

Neil cocked his head, making sure his friend wasn't messing with him. "We've got a few almost ready. You can take that one if you want."

"Don't mind if I do. What are you doing for lunch?"

Neil pointed to a nearby fridge. "What I always do. Work."

"How about you join Brian and me over at the Lodge around noon?"

"Sounds good. Should I wear my drinking boots?"

"In a word, yes."

## CAMP SPARTAN, ARRINGTON, TN

Cal took a long hot shower methodically washing all his wounds. The damned things still hurt like a champ, but the hot water helped to soothe the pain. He had to stay out of that fucking wheelchair. His whole body was stiff. It'd be good to move around more. Plus, he had work to do.

Travis called out from the other room. "You in there, Cal?"

"Give me a minute."

Cal shut off the water and wrapped himself in a big towel. He walked into the master bedroom and found Travis, scotch glass in hand, standing next to Andy.

"The front gate guards found this guy begging like a starving dog to come in," Travis said.

Andy rolled his eyes. "Very funny. How you doing, Cal?"

"Better now. It's great to see you, brother."

Andy walked over and gave Cal a hug. "I had over sixty days of leave time stocked up so I thought I'd come visit the Music City, maybe hit a couple honky tonks."

"Seriously, man," Cal said. "What are you doing here?"

Andy looked Cal dead in the eye. "If I know you at all, I know that you're planning something."

Cal looked away. "I don't know what you're talking about."

"You're planning to go after this Dante guy."

"Why the fuck do you care?"

"Do you even have to ask?"

"So what? Are you here to stop me?" Cal balled his hands into fists.

"Do you not know me at all, Cal? I'm here to help, you idiot."

Cal looked from his former platoon commander over to Travis. "You don't look too surprised."

"I *am* your cousin, Cal." Travis held out his hands. "Plus, you know how we take care of family around here. Your dad started that."

Cal's voice was soft now. "Yeah."

"So, what's the plan, cuz? What do you need from the company?"

"Trav, I really don't want to involve the company. Could you imagine what would happen simply if the media finds out that I'm involved? There'll be a real shitstorm."

"You think this is our first rodeo, cowboy? Look, I'll give you the benefit of the doubt because you've been off serving in the Corps for a while, but SSI has evolved. We've taken what your dad started to a whole new level."

"What are you talking about?"

"Corps Justice."

Now Cal was really confused. He knew the company had gone off the reservation at select times in the past, but now it sounded like there'd been a lot more happening than he'd known.

"You wanna explain or do I have to pry it out of you?"

"We've been doing a lot more work under the radar in recent years," Travis explained. "Mostly domestic stuff against terrorist cells and organized crime, but the calls keep coming. The shitheads are coming out of the woodwork."

"You said the calls keep coming? From who?"

"You name it. Your Dad had a whole network of contacts that I didn't even know about until they started calling me after your parents were killed."

"I'm still confused. Who are these people?"

"Everyone from former presidents and CIA officials right on down to local law enforcement. Shit, I had to have Neil build me a whole new secure database so I could somehow track them all. And the list just keeps growing."

Andy was suddenly intrigued. "Wait, so these contacts hire you to do wet work or something?"

"They don't hire us, per se. It's more like they inform us of something they've caught wind of, you know, just sort of casually mention it, then look the other way."

"How the hell haven't you been caught?"

Travis laughed. "Are you shitting me? I may be a SEAL but I'm not an idiot. The team Cal's dad built around here is more like family. Haven't you noticed that most of us are second-chancers? I don't know of any other corporation in the world that has employees that would literally lay down their lives for the team."

"Sounds like the Marine Corps," Andy said.

"Exactly. Uncle Calvin took an interest in people and treated them right. He was always tough but always fair. The people he brought onboard knew he would give his own life for them. We've lived by the same rules since he left us. This company is tighter than a clam's ass, and that's watertight."

"So, who pays for this secret work?" Cal asked.

"It's a complicated combination of systems," Travis said. "We pay for most of it, but we have other sources."

Cal quirked an eyebrow. "*We* pay for it?"

"Cuz, your dad setup a whole other division within the

company to do this stuff. With money coming in from our patents and fees, there's more than enough."

"So, the company is still financially sound?"

"Listen to you. You sound like you're thinking about taking over."

"I'm just curious, is all. Now than I'm officially out of the Corps, I'm gonna need something to do."

Travis thought about it for a minute. "What did you have in mind?"

"Well, I sure as hell don't want *your* job. You can keep that. I was thinking more along the lines of R&D but this other stuff sounds like I could make a difference."

"Funny you should mention Research and Development," Travis said. "I was talking with Neil the other day and we thought that's what you might like. In fact, it works out perfectly. Our new division actually does a lot of the initial trial work for R&D's creations. Neil's even been known to get dressed up in black and join the teams."

"You've gotta be shittin' me!" Cal said. "We can't afford to lose him!"

"Relax, Cal." Travis waved away the concern. "Neil's always hunkered down out of reach from the bad guys. We get him just close enough so he can monitor the use of the new gadgets and feel like he's part of the crew. The field teams love him."

"I'll bet they do."

"So back to the original question: what you need from the company?"

Cal took a minute to think about it. Hell, before this enlightening conversation, he thought he'd have to "borrow" the tools he'd need. "I'd like access to some of Neil's toys. Mainly surveillance stuff to start. This Dante guy is probably hunkered down somewhere and I've gotta dig him out."

"I think we can help with that," Travis said. "Neil has

some hacking software we've used in the past. One program can infiltrate a cell phone and track all calls. The fool even figured out a way to listen to the calls remotely. The damned thing is almost flawless."

"Is it something you have to load onto the cell phone?"

"Not like you'd think. He actually accesses it with some kind of laser. You can sit on a rooftop a mile away with this thing, paint the targeted cell phone, and it's yours."

"It doesn't sound like you're kidding," Cal said.

"I'm not. Don't ask me how the damn thing works. I just know it does."

"OK. I'll take one of those please."

"Alright. What else do you need?"

———

DANTE'S CALLS to New Orleans had finally paid off. Earlier in the day, a car arrived with four mean-looking bangers from down south. It was the first shipment of what would eventually be nine new men. These were some of his cousin's top enforcers. He'd owe his cousin some serious cash after all was said and done, but it would be worth it to take care of SSgt Cal Stokes.

# CAMP SPARTAN, ARRINGTON, TN

C al and the boys were holding rocks glasses with two fingers of scotch in each when Brian entered and made his way over to Cal.

"How you feeling?"

"A little sore, but better after that shower. Why didn't you tell me I smelled that bad?"

"I didn't want to make you cry."

"Hey, Doc," said Cal, "you know Travis and Neil, but let me introduce you to the rest of this motley crew. This is Captain Bartholomew Andrews. We served together in the fleet and I consider him one of my closest friends."

Andy leaned over and shook Brian's hand. "How are you, Doc?"

"I'm good, Sir. We talked over the phone at the hospital, right?"

"That was me. And you can cut the 'Sir' crap. Just call me Andy."

"Got it."

"Now" said Cal, "this other fine fellow here is the amazing former Marine Master Sergeant Willy Trent."

Brian looked up at the huge black man. "Didn't we see you at the chow hall?"

Cal laughed. "See, Trav? I told you he was sharp for a squid. Willy runs the mess hall when he's not kicking the crap out of the troops in the gym. Not only is he a professionally-trained chef from Johnson and Wales, he's also one of our martial arts and urban raid instructors."

Trent bent his hulking frame over and shook Brian's hand. "Good to meet you, Doc."

"You too, Top."

"We were just discussing our upcoming mission," Cal said.

Brian looked between Cal and the others in the room. "I'm sorry, what?"

"Let's just say I'm about to start playing out of bounds and you need to tell me right now whether you want out. You can still stick around but we'll politely ask you to leave whenever we're talking operationally."

"What you're talking about?"

Cal fixed a stare at the nurse. "It has to do with finishing the job I started in that downtown alley."

"You're talking about going after that West guy."

Cal smiled. "Well, I'm not talking about sending him a nasty letter."

"In that case, I'm thinking you're about to go *way* out of bounds."

"Listen, Doc, if you're not up to this, just say so and we'll come get you in an hour or so."

Brian stared at Cal like he was trying to make up his mind. "Can I ask a couple questions?"

"Shoot."

He pointed at Cal's glass. "First, can I have one of whatever you guys are drinking?"

"The Famous Grouse," Cal said.

"Never heard of it."

"My dad's favorite scotch and pretty much all I drink around here. We've got pallets of it."

"Sounds good."

Travis walked to the bar to get the drink for Brian.

"Next question?" Cal asked.

"Why not find the guy then alert the cops?" Brian asked.

"I'll answer that one," Travis said from the bar. "We've already been monitoring the situation through discrete channels. Believe it or not, even with the eyewitnesses, they don't have enough evidence to pin it all on West."

"Really?"

Travis raised his glass. "Welcome to our world, brother."

"How are you planning on getting away with this?"

Cal glanced at the other members of the party. Each held a loyal and conspiratorial look. "Well, apparently there's a lot that this company can do that I had no idea about until about an hour ago. Before we got here, I thought I was going to borrow some of Neil's toys and go do some snoopin' and poopin' by myself. Thanks to these guys, it looks like I won't have to do that alone anymore."

Brian's face changed to a look of disbelief. "Cal, you can't go waging some kind of private war on the streets of Nashville!"

Cal scrutinized his new friend. How well did he know this guy anyway? "Look, Doc, I can't promise things won't get dirty, but the initial plan is that we find this little shit and dump him in the laps of the local cops. I've gotta say, part of me hopes he'll fight back."

"Can I ask another question?"

"Sorry, Doc, unless it's about the scotch, that's it. Either you trust me and you're in, or you can go take a break in your room. I've made my decision and so have these guys. You're either part of the family or you're not."

Brian's eyes flashed with reserved anger as he continued.

"I'll give you the benefit of the doubt that you weren't trying to be a total prick with that last statement, and that maybe the booze is talking a bit. I was going to ask you how *I* would fit into this little operation."

Cal flashed a conspiratorial smile and nodded to the team. "I told you he wouldn't puss out, guys. He belongs here."

"Tell me you didn't just put me through some kind of test, Cal."

"What can I say, Doc? Once a Marine, always a Marine. Didn't your company gunny give you shit until he knew you weren't just another swabby?"

Brian chuckled. "Yeah. That guy rode my ass for months. Good guy though. He's one of the guys I saved."

MSgt Trent stepped forward. "Look, Doc, you might as well get it through your head that this place is a lot like the Marine Corps, including Cal's smart-ass comments. We all give each other a hard time, but in the end, we take care of one another. You've probably already heard some of the stories of some of us second-chancers."

Brian's eyes went wide as he stared at the six-foot seven mass of muscles. "You're a second-chancer too?"

MSgt Trent's chuckle sounded more like the rumble of a mountain landslide. "A former screw-up just like the rest of these boys. I had the misfortune of getting on the wrong side of a prick Major. I was working in the chow hall with Fifth Marines at the time. Long story short, turned out this guy was not only looking at kiddie porn on our government computers, he also made some inappropriate passes at my young female Marines. The guy had the balls to do it right in front of me. He was a terminal Major with close to twenty years in, so I guess he thought he could do whatever he wanted. Well, as soon as one of my Marines told me what was going on, I confronted him. He denied it in one breath, and in the next told me that even if he was doing anything, it wasn't any of my business. I told him the next time I heard about him messing with any of my Marines, he'd end up in the hospital."

MSgt Trent continued. "I hoped that would be the end of it. He wasn't that smart or lucky. A week later, I went into the walk-in freezer to get some supplies. I open the door and find this Major with his hand up the shirt of one of my female Marines pushed up against a produce rack. It was pretty obvious she'd been struggling. The prick had the nerve to tell me to leave. Instead I picked the scrawny fuck up by the front of his cammies and threw him through the door."

There was a pause before the story continued. "I'm not proud of what I did next, but he'd had his chance. Let's just say he won't ever have the option of getting a woman pregnant. The MPs showed up five minutes later and I told them the whole story. While the regimental commander was sympathetic, he couldn't ignore the fact that I assaulted a Marine officer – and robbed him of his chance to make little future Marines."

MSgt Trent gestured over to Cal's cousin. "Next thing I know, I'm getting a visit from Travis over there. He tells me who he is without getting into details, then offers me a tryout here at SSI. Needless to say, I jumped at the chance."

"And the rest, as they say, is history," Travis said grandly.

Trent nodded thoughtfully and continued. "Listen, Doc, nobody's forcing you, but if you walk away with anything today I want it to be this: This company and these guys will become your family. They're fair and will fight to the death for you once you're here. Besides that, the pay's pretty damned good too."

He smiled as he finished and took a long pull from his glass.

Travis, now visibly in the cups, picked up where Trent left

off. "I guess what we're saying Doc is that this'll be the last job you'll ever have."

Brian seemed close to reddening with embarrassment as the small group of men smiled knowingly. "Wait, are you offering me a job?"

"You're technically *not* a second-chancer, but I think your record and Cal vouching for you pretty much makes you a shoe-in," Travis said. "Plus, Neil told me he'd love to have some input from a medical combat vet on some of the life-saving gear he's developing."

The young nurse was completely floored. "No shit?"

"Well, you'd have to split the royalties from any new patents with Neil and the company, but I don't think that will be a problem. That would be on top of your salary."

Brian looked between Travis and Cal. "But you guys don't even know me!"

Travis chuckled. "Look, Doc, we've been doing this for a while. We've obviously got an eye for talent. Cal aside, everybody else around here is in the top one percent of their peer group."

"Screw you, Trav," Cal said, smiling. "What my cousin's trying to say is that we've done our homework on you. We know about your awards. We know about your perfect PFT and shooting scores. We know you're like us. I know this is a big decision, but we're all in agreement."

"What would I do about my other job?"

"Up to you," said Cal. "Would you rather be working there?"

"That's not what I'm saying," Brian said, slowly. "They've been good to me and the pay's not bad."

"Come on, Doc, nursing is a good service for humanity, but your talents are being wasted there. Besides, you really want to go back to changing bed pans after what you've seen around here?" Cal grinned. "Plus, I'll twist Trav's arm to take care of you on the salary side."

"It does look like you guys have a pretty good thing going around here," Brian said. "I guess I'm in."

Travis walked up to Brian and put his non-drinking arm around his new employee. "Then welcome to the family, my boy. I just have one more question for you. You're obviously a smart guy, super fit, a warrior. How come you didn't go to B.U.D.S and become a SEAL?"

Without pause, Brian innocently answered. "Because it only took me one time to pass the ASVAB."

The whole room exploded in laughter as Travis shook his head. "Looks like you'll fit right in around here, Doc."

———

DANTE CUT the connection on his cell phone and looked around at his newly assembled forces. "I just got the address. Be ready to go tomorrow night after I do a drive-by."

The hired guns all nodded and continued preparing their gear for the impending mission. Dante looked around the room appraising his beefed-up crew. Bullet proof vests and automatic weapons weren't cheap, but they were effective. Things were about to change. A war was coming.

*That Marine's about to feel some pain.*

# CAMP SPARTAN, ARRINGTON, TN

The newly formed team spent the following days going over "borrowed" police reports, courtesy of Neil.

"Someday you're gonna have to show me how the hell you find this stuff, Neil," Travis said.

"It's called plausible deniability, Mr. CEO. If I don't tell you, you can honestly tell your interrogators that you had no idea how I got my hands on this stuff. Besides, I can't show you all my secrets."

"Fair enough. How about you give us a quick rundown of what we're looking at. My eyes are starting to hurt."

"OK, here's the gist." Neil waved a hand at the reports. "The local authorities haven't come up with much. I will give them credit though; they've put a lot of resources into this investigation. Based on what Cal has told us, it looks like their rendition of what happened in the alley is pretty spot on. On the other hand, their search for West is lacking. They just don't have the resources. They've beaten the bushes and interrogated this Shorty guy but haven't come up with much. This kid was a new recruit and didn't have much knowledge of West's hideouts and operations. What they have gotten from him, they've exploited pretty efficiently."

"So, what you're saying is that we don't have much to go on," Cal said.

"Right," Neil said. "I've gone over everything they have and it really doesn't give us much help on finding West."

Cal turned to MSgt Trent, who was carefully studying a map of the Nashville area. "What do you think, Top?"

Without turning away from the map, Trent answered. "I think we need to start beating some bushes too. I'll volunteer to start on the north side of town."

"No offense, Top, but you're not the most inconspicuous of detectives," Cal said.

"Don't worry about me, Cal. What my size lacks in subtlety it more than makes up for in intimidation. I figure West is probably not only in deep shit with the cops, but also with some of his customers and rivals. The way these guys work, they're all thinly connected by financial obligations and past favors. I'll just pretend I'm looking for Mr. West to pay back the money he owes me. I can be pretty convincing when I want to be."

Cal relented. "OK. Can't say I have anything better. Neil, what do you think?"

"I'm with Top. We need to get some boots on the ground. He'll blend in best in that area anyway. I can give him some help with some gadgets if he wants. Just let me know what you need, Top."

Cal turned to his cousin. "Trav, I know you're busy but can you spare some time to talk with some of your contacts within the Metro Nashville Police Department?"

"No problem. I'll see if I can swing a lunch with a couple of my buddies. We've made some good friends on the force around here. They've even spent some time in our simulators and on our live fire ranges."

"Good. See what you can find out about on-going operations to find West and make sure they don't think we're jumping into this thing."

Cal turned to Brian next. "That leaves me, Doc, and Andy."

"OK," said Brian. "What are we doing?"

"Now that I'm getting around on my own power, I want to go have a little talk with Irene."

"The girl at your condo?"

Cal nodded. "I have a bad feeling that her walk through my condo wasn't just casual curiosity. Anybody have any other questions, comments, or concerns?"

Travis raised his hand. "Yeah, we may have one small issue. Just got a text from our legal department. Seems as though we've gotten a couple of inquiries from some local reporter. He was trying to find you and was looking for a comment on the investigation."

"Just tell them to blow him off," Cal said.

"I did but I've heard about this guy," Travis said. "He's a tenacious fucker. Young and ambitious. Gave the local police hell earlier this year over some alleged abuse scandal. Turned out to be nothing, but it really gave the police a black eye. This guy smells a story."

"What's his name?" Cal asked.

"Henry Bellinger."

"Why do I know that name?"

Travis shrugged. You've probably seen his name on any story condemning conservatives, the military, or the police. He loves conspiracies and is smart as hell."

"So how do we deal with this guy?"

"Let me think about it. I may just put the Hammer on it."

Brian looked at Travis. "The Hammer?"

"Otherwise known as Marjorie Haines. She's our lead attorney. Don't call her Hammer or she'll kick your ass."

Cal thought about the problem for a minute. "What if I give him an interview over the phone? What could that hurt?"

Travis shook his head. "No way, Cal. This prick will find some way to twist your words. He's already suggesting that you should be arrested for the murder of those guys in the alley."

Cal's anger boiled over. "Any idiot can see that my actions were in self-defense. What's he trying to prove?"

His cousin answered by pointing his finger at Cal. "That's what he's trying to prove: you're some kind of animal that should be caged. He hates the military and would love to get a juicy story on the Killer Marine. I'm saying that if you get on the hook with this guy he'll make that famous short fuse of yours to burn out really quick."

Taking a labored, calming breath, Cal nodded to his cousin. "Touché. Guess it's pretty easy to hit my hot spot sometimes."

"Yeah, well, even your dad wasn't perfect there either," Travis said. "He had a killer temper on that rare occasion he got riled."

"Tell me about it. Alright, I'll stay away from this reporter and let you handle him. You guys ready to go?"

Everybody nodded and headed for the door.

————

DANTE DROVE by the home without turning his head, but instead used his peripheral vision to take in the details. The property was probably a couple of acres and far removed from any neighbors. It was situated in the Leipers Fork area in the city of Franklin, TN. The area was known for the mansions of some of country's oldest and brightest stars.

This home was nothing like the homes of the stars. It was

a modest one level with a three-car garage. No frills. The driveway was lined with neatly spaced trees and the lawn was well maintained. Basic.

Dante drove a little way past the property and looked back. There didn't seem to be any activity outside. He decided to take a chance and pull into the vacant land adjacent to the target property. A densely wooded entryway gave him a perfect opportunity to conceal the late model Honda Civic he was driving.

Carefully slipping out of the car, he pulled down his ball cap and checked his aviator sunglasses to make sure his face was properly hidden.

He didn't have to go far to find a decent spot behind a tree that afforded him a clear view of the whole property. From the distance he couldn't see any movement. He pulled out a pair of small sport binoculars he'd purchased for cash at a nearby gas station. His eyes adjusted and focused onto the side window that seemed to be part of the living area. All he wanted at this point was to confirm that the owners still lived at the location and were alone. The last thing he wanted this go-around was more surprises.

He waited ten, twenty, thirty minutes. Nothing. Just about the time he'd decided to leave and come back, Dante caught a flicker of activity in the back of the house. *Please don't have a big fucking dog.* Dante thought.

A middle-aged man walked out the back door onto a wooden deck trailed by a tiny Chihuahua. Dante watched as the man waited for the dog to relieve itself. Finished, the small dog ran happily back into the house and man followed. *One here. Now I've gotta make sure Mama's home too.*

He shifted his gaze and, minutes later, saw what he'd waited for. The man's wife walked into view after opening the garage door. Dante focused on the two modest vehicles and didn't find the telltale signs of a family trip or impending visitors. It looked like the couple would be at home tomorrow, alone.

He took his time walking back to the car. He ran the details of the upcoming assault through his head. This time he'd be the one leading the way just like the old days. Things wouldn't go wrong this time.

# GULCH DISTRICT, NASHVILLE, TN

The three companions exited and headed for the front door of Cal's condo building. Through the glass, Cal could see Irene sitting at the welcome desk. A deep breath, and he passed through the doorway.

Irene looked up with her courtesy smile and yelped in surprise as she recognized Cal. "Well, well, look here! Cal! How are you?"

Cal noticed that the look of shock mingled with a hint of guilt on Irene's face. This girl was hiding something. Years of learning when junior Marines were lying to his face had honed his bullshit detector. He put on the nicest smile he could muster and pushed forward.

"Hey, Irene. How are things around here?"

"You know, occasionally busy, boring the rest of the time. You look great! How are you feeling?"

"A lot better, thanks. Just wanted to stop by and get some of my stuff. Oh, my fault. You've met my buddy Brian here and this is my friend Andy. Andy's a buddy of mine from the Marine Corps. They do all the heavy lifting while I just point to things."

Irene laughed dutifully, as did the others. The strain on the woman's face intensified as she processed the trio. "Are you... moving out or something?"

"Nope. Just gonna stay with some friends for a few days. Anybody been in my place since the last time I was here?"

Irene shook her head. "No, just your friend Brian the other day. I've got a bunch of mail for you. I can go get it for you and you can pick it up on your way out."

Cal looked over his shoulder. "Andy, can you go with Irene and get my mail? We'll be back down in five minutes."

"No problem," Andy said.

As Irene turned to head to the mailroom, Cal touched his right temple and glanced at Irene's desk. Andy followed his gaze, saw the cell phone, and nodded back to Cal. It would be Andy's job to use Neil's laser gadget to tap Irene's phone. Not a problem.

Cal and Brian headed to the bank of elevators and boarded the first to appear. As the doors closed, Brian turned to Cal. "You think it'll be as easy to do as Neil said?"

"Probably easier," Cal said. "By the time we get the mail, Neil should have her whole system tapped."

They were both anxious to hear from Neil and continued the rest of the way up to Cal's floor in silence, each wondering quietly what the cell phone hack would lead to.

As Cal was entering his pass code, his cell phone buzzed. He answered it on the second ring. "Yeah."

"Hey, we just got a positive connection and we're starting to download all her recent activity."

"OK. Call me back when you have a better idea of what we're dealing with."

"You got it."

Cal slipped his phone back in his pocket and walked toward the master bedroom. He came back a minute later with a small rolling suitcase. "You ready?"

"Do you need to get anything else?" Brian asked.

"Nope. Just got some extra pieces from the locker and some clothes. The rest I can borrow from the company."

Brian grabbed the suitcase and followed Cal back to the elevator. As they exited on the ground level, they found Andy waiting with a thin stack of junk mail. Irene was once again sitting behind the welcome desk, texting. She looked up as they walked toward Andy.

"Did you get everything you needed, Cal?" Her voice was still a little too bubbly.

"I did. Hey, Irene, has anyone been here recently looking for me?"

She did her best to keep the fake smile plastered on her face, but Cal noticed her face drop slightly at his questioning.

"Just the police. They came by the day after your... incident."

"Anybody else that you can remember?"

"No. I see everyone that comes in during the day. You know that the doors are locked after-hours and on the weekend."

"Yeah. I was just curious. Thanks again for keeping an eye on things, Irene."

"No problem," Irene said. "Let me know if we can do anything for you."

He started to leave, then paused and turned back. "Oh, forgot to mention one thing. Give the staff a heads-up that I installed a video surveillance system a few weeks ago. Nothing to worry about. I haven't had a chance to review any footage since getting out of the hospital yet. Just thought you guys should know."

Without waiting for a response from the open-mouthed Irene, he exited through the front door trailed by his two friends.

Andy waited until they'd reached the car before saying

anything. "Real discreet, Cal. I wouldn't be surprised if she has a heart attack."

"Serves her right. I'm tired of sitting back and doing nothing. I guarantee she'll be on the phone with whoever she's been talking to as soon as we take off. In ten minutes, we'll know where West is hiding."

Without a good response, the other two climbed into the car and they were soon back on the road to Camp Spartan.

———

DANTE STROLLED into the dark room, shedding his layers of disguise as he went. The twelve men waiting were in various states of relaxation. Some were slumped on one of the couches smoking; others were playing video games or snacking on a huge bag of Popeyes takeout.

"All right, listen up," Dante said. "I just took a look at the house we're hitting tomorrow. I figure we can get in and out pretty quickly. I don't want to be there more than five minutes in case some hillbilly decides to stop by with his shotgun. No shooting unless we can help it. Everybody got that?"

A chorus of mumbled agreements answered.

"Good. Now, I want all of you to get some good rest tonight. I don't want anybody draggin' ass tomorrow night. That means go easy on the booze and weed."

One of the huge men from New Orleans raised his head and spoke up in a bored southern drawl. "This ain't our first rodeo, Dante."

"I know, I know. I just don't want any fuckups this time."

Someone else called from the back. "You mean not like the way Shorty went down?"

The comment was followed by snickers from the rest of the hired crew.

Dante growled his response. "You trying to challenge me? If you've got a problem, I'll take care of it right now."

The guy from the back was still smiling. "Relax, boss, I was just messin' with you."

Dante turned and headed for the back room. The sooner he could send the New Orleans bangers back home, the better. The walls of the small house were starting to close in on everyone. Just the day before, one of his original crew had gotten into it with one of the newcomers. It would've come to blows if Dante hadn't happened to walk in. He was tired of babysitting.

No matter. Tomorrow would be the night it would all end.

# CAMP SPARTAN, ARRINGTON, TN

Cal, Andy and Brian arrived back at Camp Spartan to find Neil helping himself to the liquor in Cal's suite. On the bar, he'd arrayed an assortment of laptops, high tech headphones and speakers, and half-eaten room service. As Cal walked in the door, he saw Neil listening intently into one side of the set of headphones perched on his head. His concentration was so deep that he didn't even acknowledge the trio's entrance. Neil remained this way for another minute, then his eyes shot open and he ran his fingers deftly over the keyboard, apparently making notes from what he'd just listened to.

"Well?" Cal asked.

"Hold on a sec," Neil said in a flat tone, typing furiously.

Cal walked around the bar and pulled a beer out of the fridge. He motioned to the other two with the beer and both nodded. He pulled two more bottles out of the fridge, expertly popped off the tops on the side of the bar, and brought them around to Andy and Brian.

Andy waited patiently with a look of quiet amusement as Neil wrapped up his note-taking. Brian walked to the large

bay window and took in the beautiful day. Cal tr
over Neil's shoulder just for a glimpse of what h
but Neil shooed him away.

Finally, Neil finished and swiveled his bar stool around to
face the others. "OK," he said with a sigh, "I've got bad news
and good news."

Cal was impatient. "Would you just tell us what you found
out, dammit?"

"Patience is a virtue, my boy. Anyway, the good news first.
Your girl Irene has not been tipping off Dante West or any of
his crew."

"And the bad news?"

"She's been doing spy work for that reporter, Bellinger."

"What?"

"Looks like little innocent Irene is a little short on cash
and this guy Bellinger loves good contacts within the ranks of
hotel and condo concierge," Neil said. "They've usually got
the most access, so he targets them pretty heavily."

"What was she rooting around my place for?"

"Any little tidbits he could use to write a story. Your Navy
Cross citation to start. He wanted her to see if you were
maybe a druggy, closet gay, or something like that. Anything
to make his story juicier."

Cal growled. "I'd love to pay that guy a little visit."

Andy shook his head. "You know you can't do that, Cal.
It'd just make things worse. Besides, you said that from the
surveillance video you watched, she couldn't find anything."

"It still pisses me off."

"I know but listen to this." Neil's gestures became more
animated. "So, it looks like this Bellinger guy is desperate for
intel. By the tone of his voice over the phone, it's pretty
obvious he's grasping at straws. Who knows, maybe he'll give
up soon."

"I doubt it," Cal said. "He'll keep digging until he finds

something. I'll just have to be careful about being seen in public doing something stupid."

Brian couldn't resist. "When you say stupid, do you mean like hunting down a fugitive and leaving him hog-tied for the cops?"

"Yeah I guess we just need to make sure we don't get caught."

Brian groaned. "You can say that again."

It was obvious Brian still wasn't convinced the operation could be pulled off without the authorities or this reporter finding out. He took a pull from his beer.

Cal could see the apparent discomfort on Brian's face. "Have a little faith, Doc. You haven't seen any of us in action yet. I think you may be pleasantly surprised."

"That's what I'm afraid of," Brian said wryly, "actually enjoying this shit."

———

THE TEAM of four spent the next couple hours running through Irene's cell phone logs and recent text, email, and phone conversations. Other than the dialogue with the reporter, she seemed like any other twenty-something working girl.

Cal yawned as he looked at his watch. "Alright guys, why don't we break until tomorrow morning? By then, Top should be back and we may have a little more insight into the location of our beloved bad guy."

"Sounds good to me. I'm beat." Andy stretched and headed for the door. "I'll see you ladies in the morning. Anyone wanna join me for a little motivating PT run at the crack of dawn?"

Brian perked up at the mention of physical activity. "I'll go with you."

Cal laughed. "I don't think you know what you're getting into, Doc. Good ol' Andy is a marathon runner. I remember how he used to take our whole platoon on these God-awful runs. You look at the man and he doesn't look like a runner, but I've never seen anyone beat him in distances over five miles."

"I think I'll take my chances," Brian said. "I could use a solid ass-kicking after eating all this good food you guys have around here."

Andy feigned innocence. "Don't worry, Doc, I'll *try* to be nice. I'll come get you in the morning."

The rest of the team packed up and headed to their respective rooms. Cal took a minute to gaze out the window and imagine what the next day would hold. *We've gotta find that guy, dammit.* And with that, he walked to the master bedroom and fell into a fitful sleep.

# TOP

M Sgt Willy Trent was no stranger to the dark streets. Growing up in Atlanta, he'd quickly found that his premature growth spurt elicited a certain amount of respect among the neighborhood kids. Even the teenagers five years older than young Willy often deferred to his ever-growing stature.

He'd found a love for weight lifting and sports at a young age. His size was an obvious advantage on the football field and the basketball court. Unlike a lot of kids that grow quickly and have a hard time dealing with the awkwardness of clumsy long limbs, young Willy seemed gifted with natural balance and athleticism.

His size and talent quickly led him to lord over most of the young toughs in the neighborhood. Typical of adolescent mischief, fights were common. Nothing too violent, just a couple of boys punching each other, one usually walking away with nothing more than a bloody nose or soon-to-be black eye.

Because of his size and quickness, Willy never lost a fight before the age of fifteen. Up until then, he could do no wrong. The only thing he didn't succeed in – and it wasn't because he couldn't – was school work. His mind was focused only on playing sports and running his neighborhood crew. Later in life, his mental ability would be tested, and Willy wasn't too surprised to find out that his IQ was in the ninety-fifth percentile. It was this ability that made him a natural leader and crafty athlete. Brains plus brawn were a mighty combination.

At the time, Willy made it a habit to sneak out at night (and infuriate his poor mother to no end) to hang out with his friends. They'd never do any real damage, just roam the streets hooting and hollering like kids do.

It was on one of these occasions that Willy's young crew encountered one of the local punks and his small gang of hoods. Typical of Atlanta summer nights, the air was thick with humidity and a lot of kids would hang around the local 7-Eleven, sipping ice-cold Slurpees and trying to stay cool.

On this particular night Willy's crew got to the 7-Eleven after the older and larger gang led by Leshon Braxton. Leshon was in his early twenties and ran the gang with an iron fist. No one in the local neighborhood wanted to get on Leshon's bad side.

As was typical when walking the streets, Willy led the way. He recognized Leshon and nodded in acknowledgement. Leshon's eyebrows rose as he appraised the towering teen.

"Hey there, Willy!" Leshon said. "I saw you on the football field last week. Helluva game, brother."

Willy stayed quiet, nodded his thanks and continued on his path toward the front door of the store. "Hey, Willy, what's wrong? Don't you want to talk to me?"

A couple of the older boys snickered as they watched their leader egg Willy on. The tall young man turned to face Leshon. "It's all good, Leshon. Me and my boys just wanted to go get something to drink."

"OK, but that can wait a minute. Why don't you boys head on in there and get your drinks? Give me a minute to talk with Willy."

The younger boys looked to Willy for guidance. He nodded his consent and moved aside as they filed into the store.

Leshon waited until they were out of earshot to start talking again. "So how come you've never come to hang out with me and my boys, Willy?"

"You know how it is, man. These guys have been my friends since I was little."

Leshon nodded paternally. "I get it. I get it. But you know what, you're not getting any younger. Maybe it's time for you to upgrade to the big boy crew. What do you think, Willy?"

Willy knew this day would come. One of the problems with his size and ability he'd been gifted with was that he'd become a target. Some older kids searched him out because they thought he would be a good conquest. Others, like Leshon, seemed to prize Willy because they saw the strength and intelligence in the young man.

Young Willy recognized the look in Leshon's eyes. He wanted a new recruit. It'd happened before with less capable crews, but Willy got a bad feeling staring back at Leshon. He didn't seem like the type of dude that would take no for an answer.

"I don't know, man. My mama wouldn't really want me hangin' out with older guys."

At his comment about his mother, the older boys laughed out loud. One of the problems with being the target was that you just had to stand there and take it sometimes. There's no way he could match the six guys either in an argument or a fistfight. He'd just have to sit there and accept it.

"Don't you worry about your mama, Willy," Leshon said. "I'll take care of her. I'll take *good* care of her."

Leshon punctuated the lewd comment by licking his lips lasciviously.

Willy took a calming breath trying to stave off the inevitable boiling over of his anger. He wasn't the best at listening to his mother's lectures, but he was very protective of the widow. His father had died in a factory accident when Willy was three and the boy had made it his mission to protect his mother ever since. *Calm down, Willy. Getting mad will only make things worse.*

"Come on, Leshon. Can I just go inside now?"

Leshon's eyes grew wide. "You telling me what to do now, Wee Willy?"

Willy was desperate now. "No, man. I just need to get back home before my mama notices I'm gone."

"I told you, Willy, I'll take care of that fine mama of yours."

He smirked as he looked around at the matching grins on his crew. Leshon wasn't going to let him out of this.

"What do I need to do so I can go, Leshon?"

"You can start by not being a little bitch," Leshon said. "Is that what you are, Wee Willy? A little bitch?"

Willy's head snapped up. Even his tolerance for mockery had its bounds. Later in life, friends would comment that he was like a friendly giant; kind to a fault and slow to anger, but once riled he could not be stopped.

Leshon smiled at the incensed youth. "Now I see that fire, boy. How about we see how that fire burns? What do you say you and me go a couple of rounds?"

A stirring began in Willy's gut. Leshon was famous for his street brawls. He'd sent a couple of kids to the hospital, and it was rumored he'd once been a semi-pro boxer in his old hometown. Leshon was definitely built like a heavyweight fighter: standing six foot three and well into the middle two hundreds. He was an imposing figure to most other kids.

But Willy wasn't as easily deterred. Even at fifteen, he was already close to six foot four and just over two hundred pounds. Added to his formidable size were the countless hours of honing his body to athletic perfection on the football field and in the weight room. Willy was confident in his abilities one-on-one.

But not six-on-one.

"I don't wanna fight you, Leshon." His voice was a whisper.

"I didn't ask what *you* wanted, boy! Now get your ass around the back of this building and let's see who the big dog is around here!"

Leshon's companions whooped a cry of delight and pushed the reluctant Willy toward the other side of the building. Their leader led the way as he pulled off his shirt showing off an impressive array of tattoos.

Willy glanced back to the store and noticed his friends peering out of the window; wide-eyed and realizing he was in big trouble.

As the small gang reached the back of the building, Leshon turned suddenly and landed a wide right hook into Willy's left cheek. He'd seen it at the last possible second and was able to minimize the hit by turning his head to the right, but holy hell did it hurt. The blow spun Willy to the right and down to his knees. He couldn't help it.

Leshon kept taunting him. "Come on, you little bitch! Get up and show me what you got!"

*Well, there's no way out of this now.* Willy thought. He shook his head once and stood up to his full height. In that second, something in his demeanor changed. Leshon noticed it and so did the others. Willy's look of supreme confidence and cold anger caused a hush in the small crowd and made Leshon think twice about charging.

Willy used the pause to make his move. He bum-rushed

Leshon and swung a right-handed haymaker. Only it was a calculated ruse, for just as he was about to connect with his attacker's blocking arm, however, he used his momentum to hug Leshon into the path of his forehead. There was the sound of cracking shells as Willy's forehead connected with Leshon's exposed nose. Blood splattered from the flattened nostrils as the two young men fell to the ground.

Willy knew he had him. One of the things he'd learned in his early fights was that despite the rage he mustered to take out an opponent, his mind stayed serenely calm. It was yet another gift that would serve him well later in life.

He used that talent to quickly weigh his options. If he incapacitated Leshon now, he'd most likely have to turn and take on the other five. Not the best opportunity for getting out of the mess relatively unscathed. Just as he Willy cocked back to headbutt him again, Leshon screamed in fear.

*"Get this motherfucker off me!"*

The next three minutes were a complete blur as the remaining crew members jumped into the fray. Fists flew and boots stomped as the gang pounded away at the defenseless Willy. He balled up in a fetal position to protect himself.

At some point, between blows to the head and torso, Willy heard his mother's voice. She was screeching at the other young men. He looked up through bloody eyes to see his mother holding his father's old shotgun. He didn't even realize his mother knew how to use the weapon.

She leveled the shotgun at Leshon. "I'm giving you boys two seconds to get the hell out of here or I'm gonna shoot."

"This ain't over, bitch!" Leshon yelled back as he quickly fled the scene. His crew followed close behind. No one turned a head back.

"You OK, son?"

Willy raised his bloody face and looked up at his mother. In the limited light, she reminded him of a guardian angel. A shotgun-wielding guardian angel. He tried to answer, but the words came out as a slur. It was now obvious that his jaw was broken and he'd sustained other injuries to his whole body. He felt like his entire high school football team had literally run him over. Twice.

"Come on, son," his mother said. "Let's get you to the hospital. Don't try to talk."

It wasn't easy for Willy's mother to help her son off the ground, but they somehow made it vertical and around the side of the building to her idling car.

Willy later found out that one of his friends had called Mrs. Trent as soon as Leshon had provoked the fight. Luckily, the Trent household was right around the corner.

He remembered the look on his mother's face as she nursed the beaten and bruised Willy. There was a sadness there that he couldn't place. At the same time, he saw a deep determination in her eyes. He didn't know what it was until days later when his mother came in and announced that they were moving across town to live with his grandmother.

"I should've seen it a while ago, Willy," she said. "In this neighborhood, you're gonna get nothing but trouble. I've already talked to the private school across town and they say that, with a partial scholarship for football, they can put us on a payment plan. I've already talked to my cousins over there and they're gonna help me get extra work."

"I don't want you to do that, Mama. I can handle things around here."

"It's not in your control, son. You don't get nowhere fast with a target on your back. If it's not those boys that attacked you the other night, it'll be someone else. We've outgrown this town. We need to start a new life in a better place."

It was obvious to Willy that there was no use arguing. Her mind was made up and he'd have to go along with her decision. Deep down, he knew she was right. He would always be a target.

The move proved to be surprisingly easy. It was good to be close to family and Willy quickly excelled at school. The mostly-white high school was amazed at his talent on the football field. With the help of some very diligent teachers, Willy soon caught up to, or surpassed his peers in the classroom. He learned to love his studies and eventually became not only captain of the football and basketball team but also senior class president and valedictorian.

Not a bad rise for a walking target.

———

MSgt Trent thought back to those days as he strolled the streets of North Nashville. It'd been a while, but most inner city neighborhoods had a similar smell and feel. Dressed in dark clothing with a long leather trench coat, he was glad he'd never have to live in such a place ever again. *Thanks to Mama,* he thought as he said a silent prayer to his now-deceased guardian angel.

His mission was clear: infiltrate the area and get intel on the location of Dante West. He and Cal had agreed that it would be highly unlikely that Trent would stumble on West. They just needed some better information so they could hopefully triangulate the guy's whereabouts.

So far, he'd questioned a couple of winos and hookers. They'd all said the same thing: Dante hadn't shown his face in a while. He changed tactics and started pushing the fact that West owed him some big money and he was going get paid tonight or heads would roll. It was time to light a fire and see what came running out of the woods.

He finally hit pay dirt around two in the morning. One of the hookers, obviously high on something, had led him to one of Dante's supposed drug houses. Trent snuck around the side of the dilapidated duplex trying to get a better feel for what he was up against. He pulled his Beretta out of his coat pocket just in case.

Making his way to the back of the house, he heard a television through the open window. Obviously, the inhabitant wasn't trying too hard to keep the space secure. He glanced in through the corner of the window and saw two black men sitting on a dirty couch watching television and enjoying some weed. Bottle-shaped brown paper bags sat pinned between them. Both men had pistols within arm's reach on the couch. Clearly, they weren't completely stupid.

Keeping a low profile, Trent shifted his gaze around the room and saw two women sprawled naked on the floor on top of soiled blankets. Both women were passed out and probably high by the looks of their slack jaws. He didn't see any other visitors and wondered what was upstairs.

He squatted down next to the house and reached into his other coat pocket. He pulled out the small box Neil had given him. Opening the box, he extracted the pair of sunglasses and then gently handled the tiny flying spy camera. *Better safe than sorry*.

He put on the sunglasses and pressed the side arm. The tiny drone went airborne and the left lens mirrored the camera's point of view. He directed the camera to fly up to the second story window. The slight buzzing was completely muffled by the sound of the television and nighttime noises. As it came up to the second level, the drone slowed and hovered. Trent peered into the darkened room and looked through night vision eyes at the empty floor.

The device moved into the room and rotated to give Trent a full view of the contents. Lots of trashed furniture but no people. He completed the scan of the upstairs by directing the drone into the bathroom and a second bedroom. Empty. *Good.*

Next, he directed the spy camera down the stairs and into the kitchen. Other than a sink and table full of used to-go cartons, the place was empty. That left the two pushers and their girlfriends in the living room.

He brought the drone back outside and stowed it and the glasses in his pocket. After a second to think, he knew the easiest way to find out what he needed was to just knock down the back door. He was pretty sure he could take care of the two men.

He stashed his pistol back in its holster, then withdrew two more of Neil's presents. They were specially modified tasers. They were a lot smaller than the commercial version used by police and private citizens, but just as powerful. In Trent's hands, they each looked like matching Pez dispensers, roughly the same size as their candy counterparts.

Out of habit, he checked to make sure the laser sights worked. Before leaving, Neil had suggested taking two just in case. Trent would have to remember to thank the techie for the forethought. If he was lucky, he could incapacitate both men without much noise. The last thing he wanted to do was burst into the house with guns blazing.

He stayed in a crouch as he moved around to the back of the little house. The keys to what he was about to do was overwhelming force and surprise. Having the two idiots shooting at him wouldn't do any good. MSgt Trent was hoping he'd catch the men with drug- and alcohol-slowed reflexes. He took two more settling breaths, squared himself to the back door and pictured the two men ten feet from the rear entrance. Holding the Pez tasers loosely in each hand, he took one big step back then exploded through the door with his size fourteen boot leading the way.

The door shattered the locking mechanism and Trent

followed the door into the room. He looked down at the surprised expressions of the two drug dealers and didn't hesitate to aim each taser at their chests and depress the triggers.

Before the guys could reach for their guns, the taser wires reached out. The probes penetrated their thin shirts and instantly started pouring voltage into their nervous systems. Trent held down the switches for five seconds then released. The shocked duo slumped back down on the couch.

Without hesitation, the former Master Sergeant started the interrogation. "Where's Dante?"

The first man cried out shakily. "What?"

"I said, where's Dante? You don't start answering my questions and I'm gonna keep shocking."

"No, *please*..."

Trent switched on the electricity and watched as the men writhed in agony. Turning the juice off, he started again.

"Like I told you," Trent said, "answer my questions. Now, one more time: Where's Dante?"

The first man spoke again. "I don't know, man!"

The next shock threw the man's head back, hitting the wooden frame of the couch with a sharp crack. Turning off the power again, Trent explained calmly, "I'm gonna tell you this one last time. Dante owes me some money and I mean to get it tonight. The only thing I want you boys to tell me is how I can find the motherfucker."

The second man finally spoke. "OK, OK!"

Despite the screams and grunts, neither of the passed-out women on the floor had yet to stir.

"You ready to tell me where he is?" Trent asked.

"We don't know exactly where he is," the second man said. "He's been moving around a lot."

"You mean since he killed that girl?"

"I don't know anything about that, man. All I know is

that the cops are after him and we haven't seen him for a while."

"So how do you know he's still around?" Trent asked.

"He calls us a couple of times a day. Dante wants to make sure we're still making money for him."

"Does he call you on your cell phone?"

"Yeah." The man motioned with his head at the end table where two new mobile phones sat in chargers. "Usually calls once in the morning and once at night. Wants to know how big our haul was."

"And how was your haul today?" Trent asked.

The man looked at his companion not knowing how he should answer the hulking trespasser.

"Wrong answer, dipshit!" Trent depressed the power switch, again wondering how many times he'd have to do it. After a good long shock, he turned off the power. "How was your haul today?"

The second man answered again, despite his trembling. "Dammit, man! It was good, OK? You know what kind of trouble we're gonna be in with Dante for telling you this shit?"

"Don't you worry about Dante. I don't think he's gonna be around much longer. I've heard I'm not the only one looking for money. I just want to be the first one to get mine."

"You can take whatever we've got here, just don't tase us again, man!"

"How much do you have?" Trent asked.

"A couple grand."

"A couple grand?" Willy said, laughing. "I thought you said you had a good haul today."

"We did," the man said, "but Dante sends one of his girls to come pick up every night. She usually comes by around midnight."

Knowing he had to keep up the charade, Trent went in another direction. "OK, where's the money you have here?"

The man on the left pointed to a Nike shoebox on the floor. "In there."

"A safe deposit box. Very intelligent. Alright, you two sit tight as I make sure you're not bullshitting me."

Keeping the two men directly in front of him, Trent shifted around and glanced down into the box. It definitely looked like there was a couple of thousand dollars in assorted bills piled neatly inside.

"Here's what's gonna happen next, boys," Trent said. "You're gonna turn, face each other and give one another a big hug."

The second man cocked his head to the side. "What?"

Trent didn't even bother warning the men as he depressed the taser one last time. When the jolts ceased, both men had obviously met their limit and were ready to comply.

"Like I said," Trent continued, "I want you to face each other, give your buddy a big hug, and hold it."

The two men looked at each other not really wanting to know what was coming next. They did as instructed and glared back at Trent.

"Now, you with the arms on top I want you to straddle your homeboy."

The man hesitated only briefly then awkwardly climbed onto his friend's lap with his legs and arms wrapped tightly. Trent shifted the tasers so that he had both in his left hand, then reached into a large cargo side pocket and pulled out a handful of long black zip ties.

"If either one of you fuckers move, I'm gonna shock you until you're stupid for life. Got it?" Both men nodded and didn't budge as Trent expertly tied both set of hands and feet with the cables. "I hate to do this to you guys, but I can't have you running after me. Don't worry, as soon as your ladies wake up, they can cut you out."

He linked two zip ties together and looped it all the way around both men's necks. He secured a neck restraint by looping another zip tie between the two and cinching it down tightly. They weren't going anywhere without strangling themselves – not without help from their unconscious companions.

He finished by pulling out the taser wires and stuffing them, two cell phones, and two pistols into the cardboard box full of cash.

"Well, boys, thanks for your cooperation. And remember: Just say no to drugs."

Trent exited the way he came in and slowly made his way back to his concealed pickup truck down an alley a couple of blocks away.

He pulled out his cell phone and dialed Cal, who picked up on the first ring.

"Yeah."

"I think I got one of those breaks we were looking for," Trent told him.

"OK. I'll put on the coffee and wake up the boys. I'll see you when you get back."

"Roger, out."

Trent replaced his phone, started the big diesel engine and made his way back down to the compound.

*Not bad for a former misfit*, he thought.

## CAMP SPARTAN, ARRINGTON, TN

After relaying the story – pausing once in a while for laughter – to the assembled group consisting of Cal, Brian, Andy, Travis and Neil, Trent went on to explain what he thought they should do with the stolen cell phones.

"It seems to me that West is pretty tight on cash. I doubt he'd want to miss any one of his pickups. My vote would be to set a little ambush for his cash girl and convince her to take us back to Dante tomorrow night. The problem is, now he'll know we're onto him if he calls one of these cell phones."

Cal turned to Neil. "Do you have any way to tap into these cell phones?"

"I thought you'd never ask. I can make these phones do things you could never imagine. When I'm done with them, they'll be singing like canaries."

"You wanna tell us how you're gonna do that or do I have to zip tie your ass like Top's buddies?"

Neil looked apologetic. "Didn't mean to be a smartass, Cal. So, here's what I'm gonna do. I'll take whatever info I can off the cell phones. I can pretty much guarantee they're disposables so their secrets will be limited. If we're lucky, I might be able to find the phone number West is calling from and then use the cell carrier's network to pinpoint which towers he's been feeding off of when he calls. That *might* give us a better idea of where he's operating out of. Again, no promises."

Cal nodded. "That's more than we had an hour ago. Do the best you can and get us close. I think the rest of us should get working on gear."

————

ABOUT FIFTEEN MINUTES LATER, Neil looked up from his laptop. "I've got something!"

The rest of the group crowded around to look over his shoulder. The entire screen looked like complete gibberish to all except for the excited computer hacker.

Neil pointed at the screen. "So, check this out right here. I told the program to look for the two numbers I tagged that were recently used by West. At least we know he's still in the area."

Cal stared at the screen not fully comprehending what he should be looking at. "Dude, do you want to tell us what the hell you're talking about? What is all that crap on the screen?"

"These right here are the periodic signals from the towers on the north end of Nashville," Neil explained. "All the recent pings are in the same area."

"So, we can see exactly where this guy is hiding," Brian said.

Neil shook his head. "Nope. This just shows us the general area he's hanging out in."

"How big of an area are we talking about?" Trent asked.

Neil looked sheepish. "About two square miles."

Cal clenched his fist in frustration. "That's like finding a needle in a haystack. Can't you do any better than that?"

"I told you this wasn't foolproof, Cal," Neil said. "It doesn't help that West isn't a total idiot. He's clearly utilizing multiple disposable phones and using them only when needed. The best shot we have is if he calls one of the phones Willy brought back; *or* we catch him moving out of the area he's been hanging out in."

"Shit." Cal dragged a hand down his face. "Look, we don't have much time before he realizes those cell phones are compromised. Anyone have any bright ideas?"

Andy shrugged. "What if we just give the guy a call? What's the worst that could happen? Maybe Master Sergeant Trent could play his 'give me my money' routine?"

"To what end?" Cal asked. "He'd just trash the phone he's got. No, we've gotta have a better plan to use these damn things to our advantage."

Cal picked up one of the stolen cell phones and started turning it over and over as he contemplated their next step.

"What if we get him to run?" Brian said suddenly.

Cal turned to the former Corpsman and waved for him to continue.

"What I mean is, set up some kind of loose perimeter in the area we think he's hanging out in. Then maybe Top can scare him enough to run into our net. It's not the perfect solution, but at least it's something."

It was obvious, after a few quiet seconds, that no one really loved the idea, but all were at a loss to come up with something better.

"So, let's say we get this guy out in the open," Andy said. "Then what? A *French Connection*-style chase through the streets of Nashville? I see way too many things wrong with the idea, but unless we can pinpoint his exact location and conduct a quick raid, I can't think of anything better."

Cal nodded and stroked his chin. "So, if we can't just catch him in the open, can we somehow lure him to another location and take him there?"

Trent checked his watch. "Cal, it's six in the morning and I really don't think—"

The silent buzzing of one of the confiscated phones cut off Trent's comment. Everyone looked down in anticipation as Neil carefully picked it up and looked at the caller ID.

"It's him."

Without hesitation, MSgt Trent grabbed the small phone and answered on speakerphone. "Yeah?"

"Yo, who's this?" Dante asked.

"A customer."

"Listen, asshole, put Jevon on the phone."

"Jevon ain't here. He went to take a leak."

"Then put Polo on."

"He's upstairs gettin' it on with one of the girls."

They could hear swearing in the background as Dante tried to figure out what the hell was going on. "Go get those idiots and tell them to call me back!"

The line went dead.

"Well, that buys us two minutes," Trent said. "Any ideas?"

Neil looked up from his computer. "I think I've got something. My tracking program was able to pinpoint West's location down to one square block. Is there any way we can get there fast?"

Andy shook his head. "Now that it's light out, I don't see how we can pull this off without the whole world knowing. I say we call him back and tell him we know where he is and see what happens. Cal, can we get some of your company assets up there like yesterday?"

Cal turned to his cousin. "Trav, can I get four teams of two in civvies and standard vehicles up to Nashville?"

"I'll have them out front in ten minutes."

"Let's split up into two teams. Me, Top and Neil will ride in Top's truck. Doc, can you drive your car up with Andy? I would rather keep you two a little farther back just in case."

Brian shrugged. "No problem."

"Alright, everybody grab your gear and any weapons you can conceal on your person," Cal said. "Top, do you still have some extra shotguns in the back of your truck?"

"Yeah."

"Why don't you go down with Doc and give him and Andy each one."

"You got it."

Trent, Brian and Andy left the room.

Cal turned to his tech guru. "Neil, can you bring your tracking gear on the ride with us?"

"Of course."

"Good. Now go put on some more operational shoes and let's get going."

Neil looked down at his Italian loafers. "I thought I had them on already."

———

AS PROMISED, ten minutes later the teams assembled outside the Lodge. Cal gave everyone their instructions and patrol areas. Neil handed out small water-tight boxes to each team. Cal looked at him quizzically. Neil just winked back.

No one hesitated as they jumped in their respective vehicles and headed north.

# NASHVILLE, TN

Cal looked into the back of the truck's cab to see if Neil was up and running. "You getting anything yet?"

"Nope. I probably won't get a damned thing until Top makes the next call. I'm worried this guy's gonna lose the phone and then we're shit out of luck."

"All right then, let's make the call, Top. Remember, keep him on the line as long as you. Say anything you need to."

Although he was driving, MSgt Trent pulled out the stolen cell and re-dialed Dante's number on speaker. The other man picked up after the first ring.

"Where the fuck have you been?"

"I've been in my truck," Trent said coolly.

"What do you mean, you've been in your truck? I told that fool to have you give... Wait a minute, who is this?"

"This is the fool."

"What are you talkin' about?"

"The fool you owe money to, bitch."

Dante was silent for a few seconds. "Where are my two boys?"

"Don't you worry about them. They're nice and cozy."

Dante's voice rose in anger. "Fool, if I find out you killed them..."

"Calm down, Dante. I didn't kill 'em. I'm just after my money."

"Fool, I don't even know who you are, asshole."

"Fool or asshole? Make up your mind. And I told you, I'm the one you owe money to," Trent said again.

Neil poked his arm through the two front seats with a thumbs-up signaling that he'd caught the cell phone trail. He'd silently told them that he'd need about a minute after latching on to the signal before he could get a better location. The convoy was still about ten minutes from their target.

Now West sounded amused. "If I owed you money, you'd either be dead or on a payment plan by now. I don't know you. And if I don't know you, that means I don't owe you."

Trent glanced at Cal who gave him the keep going signal. "I said you owe me. I didn't say that you know me. It was actually one of your boys that I took care of over in the shitty little house in East Nashville. Motherfucker stiffed me out of ten grand last month when I came to deliver supply. I asked him to pay me and he told me to talk to you. Something about it being *your* business."

There was a pause on the other end as Dante weighed the new information. He wasn't an idiot. He wanted to keep all the customers he could get. Gangster or not, he was still a businessman.

"Look, fool, I don't know what that idiot told you but I never stiff my customers or my competition. This town is too small for that shit."

"That's what surprised me. I've been doing business with your guys for a while and this was the first time I ever felt cheated. So, what do we need to do to get me my money back?"

Trent looked at Cal who shrugged his shoulders as if to say, *I can't believe this guy is buying this.*

"How about I have a little talk with my boy and I'm sure we can get this thing worked out."

"How about I come over to your place and we talk about it?"

"Sorry, man, that I can't do. Give me a couple minutes and I'll call you back."

Trent looked at Cal again, who nodded.

"OK. Call me back."

The line went quiet as the call ended.

Cal smacked Trent on the shoulder. "Nice job, Top. I guess he took the bait."

"Yeah, but I wouldn't count him out yet. He's like a cornered rat. A *smart* cornered rat. I could almost see the wheels in his head turning. Did you see how fast he calmed himself down? This is one cool customer."

Cal looked thoughtful. "Yeah."

"So, have you figured out what we're gonna do with this guy when we get him?"

"I figured we'd just have to see how it plays out. I'm sure, with the experience you guys have had in the past, we can hatch up some plan to dump him on the police without anyone knowing it was us."

"Now you're thinking," Trent said. "We can't let him know it's us either. That would be bad for you *and* for the company."

Neil raised a small duffel bag on the seat next to him. "Good thing we've got a bag full of black masks back here."

There was silence for a minute as Cal digested the conversation and planned the upcoming action. Worst case, they would miss West. Best case, they would find him. Then what? Cal couldn't run from what he felt in his heart: He wanted to see West die by his own hands. The realist in Cal pondered the idea and knew it wasn't the logical outcome. He could not put his people in jeopardy or endanger their livelihood. Furthermore, he did not want to be known as the wayward son that brought down his dead father's company.

*Think, Cal, think.*

He'd just come to a decision when Neil tapped him on the shoulder. "Put this in your ear, the team's checking in."

Cal glanced back as Neil handed him what looked like a miniature hearing aid. "What do I do with this thing?"

"I forgot you haven't used one of these yet," Neil said. "It's one of my latest gadgets. The boys in the field love it. It's going to let you communicate with the rest of the team. You're the only one that everyone will be able to hear all the time until you tap the side there." He pointed to the slightly raised edge on the side of the earpiece. "Tap it once to talk."

"How powerful is this thing?"

"Thanks to my mad skills, it's got a range of just over a mile. The battery is another one of my designs and will give you about twenty hours of straight use without recharging."

"Nice."

Cal slipped the tiny piece of communication gear in his left ear. He tapped the side of the earpiece.

"This is Snake Eye Six, teams check in, over."

Each of the six teams, including Brian and Andy, checked in with their respective assigned team numbers.

"OK, listen up. We're about five minutes out. When you get into position, I want your baby birds on the fly, over."

Each team confirmed. The quick plan Cal had laid out for the team prior to departure was that each pair would have one of the spy drones for easier reconnaissance. Upon final check in each team would launch their Baby Bird – Cal had named the drones much to the chagrin of Neil, who thought they should be called something more sophisticated – and discretely recon the objective. It would be tricky in the light of day, but the miniature size of the Baby Birds decreased the likelihood of detection by curious civilians.

———

"SOMETHING'S NOT RIGHT ABOUT THIS," Dante said to himself.

Two of the hired guns glanced up in confusion. Dante waved them back to their card game.

He mentally processed each of his customers and drug partners. He knew the two men running the operation that had apparently been raided by the mysterious caller. He'd made a quick call to one of his whores to go take a peek inside. The soonest she could be there was in ten minutes.

*Shit*, Dante thought. He didn't like other people having the upper hand. West didn't like owing people either. It seemed like ever since that damn thing with Shorty he was neck deep in favors. Yes, he was a criminal, but he liked to think of himself as a relatively honest criminal. His crew always delivered, and never dared tread on some else's territory unless provoked –or if it was marked for acquisition by Dante himself. By keeping that tight rein on operations, N.O.N. had seen solid growth in income and recruitment since 2005. West did not want that to go to shit. So, what should he do about this caller he supposedly owed money to?

# NASHVILLE, TN

N eil let out a victory whoop. "I've got him!"

"Where is he?"

Neil swiveled his laptop so Cal could see and tapped on the property address. Cal relayed the information to the rest of the teams: The net just got a lot tighter.

"We're five minutes out. Let's get him back on the phone just to make sure."

MSgt Trent hit redial.

Dante answered on the first ring. "Yeah?"

"Did you find out where my money is?"

"Not yet."

"That's not good, brother."

"I know, I know. Look, I'm working on it. It doesn't help that I can't get a hold of the two boys you handled."

"Not my problem, Dante. Maybe I should come by and visit."

"Look, man, I think you know that there's no way I'm gonna tell you where I am, so how about we just calm down and wait."

"I'm not so good at waiting, Dante." Trent pushed harder.

"What if I told you your boys told me where you're hanging out?"

He looked at Cal and smiled. He could hear the bastard sweating.

––––––––

THE COMMENT DISTURBED DANTE. Deep down he knew there was no way his crew had snitched. Hell, he hadn't even told them where he was hiding. He wasn't stupid.

At the same time, the paranoid part of Dante West made him peek out the front window of the house. He didn't see anything suspicious. Besides, he had a house full of firepower ready to defend himself. The problem was that he just couldn't shake the confidence of this deep-voiced caller.

"I told you, man, there's no way you know where I am," Dante said. "Give me another couple of minutes. I've got a girl going over to the house. In two minutes, I'll know which of my boys I need to squeeze to get your money."

"What if I told you I'm on my way to your place right now, Dante?"

"I'd say you're bullshitting me." West peered out the window again. The other men in the room had gone mute and were watching Dante.

"I don't bullshit, bitch. I'm gonna get my money one way or another."

West put his phone on mute and yelled at his crew. "Get up off your asses and pack your shit. I think we've got trouble coming."

The men started running around gathering their gear in a fairly organized manner. These men were not novices to danger. They already had their weapons at the ready as each headed for the back door and their escape vehicles.

Dante took his cell phone off mute. "I've had enough of

this conversation, man. Even if you are on your way, I'm gonna be gone. I'll call you from another phone later, if I feel like it."

He finished the call and began thinking faster than ever.

————

THE CONVERSATION ENDED and the line went dead.

Cal tapped on his earpiece and started instructing his assault teams. "All teams, get the Baby Birds ready. Target is on the move, I repeat, target is on the move."

It was overkill to let his men know to prepare their firearms. These were veterans who didn't hit the latrine without a weapon. They'd be ready when asked to execute. Each knew without being told that action within a civilian neighborhood required extreme caution. Firepower wouldn't be used except as a last resort. Per standard operating procedure, each member was given multiple tasers in the event close contact warranted non-lethal intervention.

As they rounded the second to last turn approaching the address provided by Neil, Cal pulled down his ball cap to conceal his face as much as possible. He didn't think wearing a black mask in a neighborhood would be the most inconspicuous disguise. Besides, he wasn't planning on letting Dante get a look at him.

The others didn't bother with the masks either. No one really thought West would call the cops and describe them to a sketch artist.

Cal heard his earpiece beep and listened to team Three.

"Six, this is Three. I think we just saw our target roll by. He's in a nineties model maroon Honda Accord. Target is driving and there are four other targets inside. Big boys too. How copy, over?"

"Roger, let's launch all Baby Birds now."

Team 2, made up of Andy and Brian, chimed in. "Six, this is Two, we've got three other vehicles leaving the target address."

"Dammit. All teams, any ideas on how to exploit this situation, over?"

There was a pause as each team pondered the question they'd already been calculating. They all knew the danger of exposing themselves. A prolonged chase and shootout was not in anyone's interest. It was Andy who spoke up first.

"Six, I think we need to go with Plan B."

Plan B was to call the local authorities and give them a good location on the wanted gang leader. Cal wrestled with the thought. He wanted nothing else but to get the man who'd killed his beloved. But how could they take the man out without engaging a bunch of armed gang members in the middle of the city?

In the desert of the Middle East, he wouldn't have thought twice. The decision would've been easy. This war was a different story. His team wasn't riding to battle in armored vehicles and combat gear. They were pursuing a wanted criminal in the heart of America wearing normal clothes and carrying a few measly weapons. Cal knew what he had to do.

"Roger that," Cal said. "I'll make the call."

Cal picked up the disposable cell phone that Neil had provided at step-off and dialed the number for Nashville's Metro Police Department. He relayed the pertinent information to the operator then hung up twenty seconds later.

His head hung down for a couple seconds and then he looked at his friends.

Trent spoke up first. "Don't worry, Cal, the cops won't get this guy. We'll find him later."

Cal nodded and looked back at his cell phone. If only he could use it to call in some artillery support or even some

30mm mortar rounds. As he daydreamed, he heard reports from the teams. West was slipping through their fingers.

"Six, Two, the cars have split up onto different roads, over."

"Six, Four, still have eyes-on target with Baby Bird, over."

"Six, Three, still have eyes on target. Target is speeding up, over." There was a pause. "Six, Three, cops just spotted target's car. Wait... lights are on, target is speeding up, over."

"Six, Two, the two cars we're following just sped up too, over."

"Six, Four, target is outpacing Baby Bird, over."

"Six, Three, trying to casually keep up with the chase, but they're really moving now, over."

Cal looked up and tapped his earpiece. "All teams break pursuit and meet-up at rendezvous point Charlie, out."

His face covered in silent frustration, Cal took the earpiece out, bent toward the console, and turned on the police scanner.

———

"WHERE THE FUCK did this guy come from?" Dante accelerated through the red light. His four passengers looked back toward the trailing police cruiser.

One minute they'd been driving down Dickerson Pike matching the speed limit, then some cop had lit them up and pulled up behind them.

Not easily scared, West was now completely spooked. First, the call from the mysterious money collector and now the cops were onto him? This was the fourth car he'd had since being on the run. All the tags were legit. The car was clean. What the hell was going on? Was it possible the guy on the phone was a cop?

As he let that thought tumble through his mind, he

continued to accelerate and speed through intersections. He swerved to miss cars and put more distance between him and the now-fading cop car. He'd had each of his escape rides specially equipped with new racing engines straight out of *The Fast and the Furious*. The cops didn't stand a chance unless they got a helicopter up above. West wasn't going to give them that opportunity.

Being the savvy criminal that he was, he'd already planned out multiple contingencies for escape. Right now, he was on his way to one of his many safe houses where he'd pick up another ride and move from there.

With the police cruiser fast fading in his rearview mirror, Dante was already finalizing his plans for the operation later that day.

————

CAL WAS silent as he listened to the police described the inevitable outcome. The police helicopter was on the other side of town when the call was placed. By the time it came on station, West had evaded the lagging police cruiser.

Trent put a reassuring hand on Cal's shoulder. "There wasn't much more that we could've done, Cal."

"I know. It just pisses me off that he was so close and we couldn't do a damned thing."

"Now you know what the cops deal with every day."

"Yeah."

"Where to now?"

"Let's head back down south," Cal said. "Neil, can you radio the rest of the guys and tell them to head home?"

"No problem."

————

THE TEAMS MET BRIEFLY outside the campus headquarters building. There wasn't much to say other than a couple thank-yous from Cal so the crowd quickly dispersed.

"I wish we could've done more," Andy said.

Cal nodded. "I know, but it was the right call. Thanks for making it."

"No problem. Hey, you know what that reminded me of?"

Cal looked confused for a second and then the light bulb went on. "That patrol we were on with the sheepherders!"

Brian looked from Cal to Andy, then back to Cal again. "You jarheads wanna tell me what the hell you're talking about?"

Andy turned to Brian and explained. "Our platoon was running one of those crappy patrols on another hot-ass Afghan day. Well, all of a sudden, Cal looks to our right and sees two insurgents peeking over a little hill about a hundred yards away. We immediately take cover and call battalion to get some fire support. We get weapons platoon on the hook and tell them what we've got. The platoon commander was a buddy of mine and told me that if I wanted to have some big guns there was a pair of Cobra gunships a few clicks away. As you probably know, it's always fun to watch the Cobras fire some rounds, so my buddy patches me through. Right about the time the gunships get on station, my radio operator taps me on the shoulder and points back to the little hill. I look over there and I'll be damned if there isn't a fucking flock of two hundred sheep strolling up to the hill flanked by a couple of herders. The two insurgents decide to take advantage of the distraction. They actually run into the middle of the herd and hunker down with the sheep."

Brian laughed. "No way."

Andy beamed. "So, the Cobra pilot gets on the hook and tells me he can see the two insurgents but that he can't shoot because of the livestock and herders. I told the guy that we suspected the two bad guys were lying in wait so they could trip an IED. The pilot didn't care. He said the rules of engagement were tight. He couldn't shoot up a bunch of local sheep because some paper pusher in the rear had decided it was bad for local relations. So what do we do? We had to just sit there and wait for the two guys to come out. We're sitting there watching as the two Cobras are literally hovering overhead, the two guys don't even shoot at them."

"I'll bet they were pissing their pants, though" Brian said.

Andy nodded. "We would've run over there except we were still waiting for EOD to get there so they could sweep the road for explosives. Well, even when the Cobras floated lower to try and scatter the sheep, the damned things stayed calm and the insurgents stayed with the sheep as they were guided toward the little town. I called everyone I could, but we couldn't get anyone else in on the ground in time and because of the IED threat. So, we had to watch these two guys mosey on into the sunset with their herd of sheep. That's what I felt like today."

Cal chuckled. "Now that I think about it, it's a pretty good comparison. Let's get back to the Lodge. I think I'm in need of a couple of fingers of The Famous Grouse."

As the friends hopped in their vehicles and made their way to the bar, Cal said a silent prayer to his beloved Jess.

*Don't worry, baby*, he thought. *The fucker's mine.*

# PART THREE

# N.O.N. SAFE HOUSE, NASHVILLE, TN

"Dante, the boys are all set and we have that van you wanted."

West stared at the hulking messenger, one of the hired guns from New Orleans. He'd especially be glad to have this guy gone soon. West wasn't afraid of much, but being surrounded by a bunch of bouncers with guns, even vouched bouncers, made him antsy.

"All right, thanks," Dante said. "Tell your boys that we'll be taking off as soon as it gets dark. I want everyone on the level. No drinking or drugs. Clear heads for this last thing."

"We ain't idiots, Dante. We'll be ready to go."

West nodded and closed the door to his new bedroom. As he looked around yet another dingy room, he dreamed of the day he could live in luxury once again. *Just a few more hours. Just a few more hours.*

———

TRENT RAISED HIS FULL GLASS. "I'm limiting myself to one of these. My ass is draggin'."

Cal raised his own in salute. "Thanks for all your help today, Top. We wouldn't have even had a chance to catch West if you hadn't tracked him down."

Trent drained his glass and looked back at Cal. "We'll get the guy, Cal. Let's all get a little shut-eye and we'll hit the streets again tonight."

"Thanks, Top."

Trent nodded and, with surprising grace considering his size, hopped up from the couch and left the bar.

Brian motioned to the bartender. Cal had told him the guy was a former Marine sergeant major who'd come onboard after losing a leg in the first Gulf War and soon became one of Cal Sr.'s first hires. The bartender nodded back and walked around the bar with a half-full bottle of The Famous Grouse. He gave everyone in the group a healthy splash finishing with Cal.

"Thanks, Sergeant Major. How's the new book coming?"

"Slowly. Took me a while to get my rusty brain running again. Neil set me up with a laptop behind the bar so I can write while I work. Thanks again for that, Neil."

Neil waved nonchalantly. "Anything for my warriors, Sergeant Major."

Andy and Brian looked on intrigued. Andy spoke up first. "What's the book about, Sergeant Major?"

"It's the story about my time in the first Gulf War and how I lost my leg."

"If I can ask, how *did* you lose it?" Andy asked.

"I was off doing some long-range recon for Cal's dad and ran into a bunch of bad guys. Me and my spotter were able to take out the guys, but not before one lucky sonofabitch lobbed a grenade our way. I'm lucky that I only lost my leg. Hurt something fierce when my spotter dragged me a couple clicks back to our evac point."

"So, what made you write the story now?"

The bartender pointed to Cal. "That young man right there. He came back from the sand pit and, after a few libations he convinced me that *someone* would want to hear my story."

"As usual, the Sergeant Major is being modest," Cal said, leveling the other man with a look. "The book isn't just about that one incident. What he failed to mention, of course, was that he got a Silver Star out of that one because the bad guys in question were on their way to ambush one of dad's companies. He and his spotter took out almost the entire enemy party of twenty some guys with a sniper rifle and an M-203. The rest of the book is gonna be about his battle to regain active duty status after losing his leg. His fight to do that will really resonate with wounded guys coming back from war today."

"Yeah, well, I guess that's where it finally got me. If the book can help even one disabled Marine, how could I say no?"

Brian slapped Cal on the back. "It's good to know that I'm not the only one that doesn't seem to have the ability to say no to our fearless leader here."

"He takes after his father that way," the bartender said. "Never could say no to Colonel Stokes either. They must have some voodoo magic in their blood or something."

Cal shook his head and responded to the obvious compliment. "No, you've got it all wrong. I've just found that it's a lot easier to convince you guys to do things when you've had a couple of these."

He raised his glass to demonstrate the proper sipping technique for The Famous Grouse.

"Well, be that as it may, I'm still glad you made me do it, Cal. I'll get you the rough draft in a couple of weeks. You can tell me whether an old salty Marine with only a high school education can actually write."

He turned back to the bar and resumed his duties as the group settled in to finish their drinks. Cal couldn't let that last comment pass.

"The good Sergeant Major is, of course, being modest again. What he fails to mention, is not only did he regain his active duty status as a Gunny, but he went on to be one of the first Marine first sergeants to serve with a line company with a prosthetic leg. Then he went on to become a Sergeant Major while also finding time to earn two masters degrees *and* PT his battalion into the dirt. Don't let him fool you with that fake limp of high school education bit. He puts on his Cheetah prosthesis and he'll give Marathon Andy a run for his money."

As the gathered crew discussed recent events, Cal's mind began to wander. He replayed the day's action over and over. What could they have done differently? What if they'd kept following West and not called the cops? He finally filed it all away for future analysis, knowing that the team had done all that was possible without blowing their cover. It didn't matter, Cal was convinced that he'd somehow find West again very soon.

———

ON THE OTHER side of town, West's crew was finalizing plans for that night's operation. No one knew the location except for Dante himself. He'd given clipped instructions to his hired muscle. Although he didn't think there would be much resistance, his recent failures necessitated extreme caution. Each man merely nodded as they listened to his orders.

———

AFTER ADJOURNING FROM THE BAR, Brian and Andy headed

back to their respective rooms. Neil and Cal headed to Travis's office to discuss options for continuing the search.

"So, what are you thinking about work-wise after we get this guy, Cal?" Neil asked.

Cal shrugged his shoulders, still not clear about where his path might lead. "I'm not sure. I want to see this thing out first, then who knows? Maybe I'll go on a long vacation."

Neil glanced empathetically at his friend as they walked. "Have you talked to Higgins yet?"

Dr. Alvin Higgins, PhD, was SSI's resident psychiatrist. He'd been a long-time member of the CIA's brain squad for years. He came to SSI after working with the company on a particularly hairy case a few years back. He was SSI's resident expert in all things intellectual, meaning he could either unwrap the mental wiring of criminals and terrorist leaders, conduct interrogations (he'd developed new and non-lethal techniques for the CIA for years), or help SSI employees and family members with any counseling they needed.

A pudgy man, a smidge over five and half feet tall, the affable Dr. Higgins had quickly endeared himself to the employees at SSI. Where some psychiatrists were aloof and borderline condescending, Higgins was the exact opposite. Jolly in a way that reminding you of Santa Claus, Higgins had actually been the reigning Saint Nick every year at company Christmas parties. Not really what you'd expect from a man who'd dedicated most of his adult life to the extraction of information from men's minds by all means necessary.

Cal shook his head. "No, I haven't seen him yet. Come to think of it, he'll probably be with Trav right now. Trav said he'd gather the inner circle to think this West thing out."

As they entered the headquarters building, the usual bustle of activity seemed like home to Cal. He'd never officially worked at SSI, but he'd practically grown up in these halls. At the same time, he always got the feeling that he was in the middle of a battalion headquarters in the field. Electronic maps and target dossiers were displayed on an impressive array of flat screen panels all along each wall. SSI remained on the tip of the technology curve; thanks, in no small part, to Neil and his team of techie geeks.

They headed to Travis' secure office. In reality, this entire building and any other SSI structure with any sort of information capability, was shielded from outside snooping by advanced electronic jamming and masking technology, once again courtesy of Neil's R&D team. The masking system was now being leased by numerous government facilities and a mobile version was also in development for field headquarters.

Cal entered Travis' spacious office not really knowing who to expect. He glanced to the eight-man conference table in the corner and found the party waiting. Two others accompanied his cousin. The group included the first female employed by SSI: company attorney Marjorie Haines. "The Hammer." Not only ferocious in court and deposition rooms, she was also an expert martial artist in Brazilian jiu-jitsu and kung fu. She'd been known to take down multiple new recruits on the fighting mat after a particularly trying day.

She'd entered SSI shortly after winning a case against the company. Travis and the rest of the executive team had been so impressed with her tenacity that they'd gone after her to fill the role of lead attorney. It didn't hurt that she could match many of the men in physical discipline, was a former prosecutor in the Navy JAG Corps, and a diehard patriot. She was, of course, well paid for her efforts at SSI and was considered one of the inner circle members. Today she was standing casually, her typical gray pant suit perfectly tailored to her athletic build. Her dark hair was pulled back in a sleek pony tail.

And next to Haines was SSI's head of internal security,

Todd Dunn. Dunn was one of Travis' first hires at SSI and a beast. If there could be a human version of an English bulldog, it would be Dunn. A muscular barrel of a man and former Army Ranger, Dunn rarely cracked a smile, but could be absolutely depended on, as anyone who knew his story could attest...

# DUNN

He had been a star in the Rangers, quickly rising through the enlisted ranks. Shortly after re-enlisting, his father had been diagnosed with cancer. Todd Dunn, now separated from his parents by a four-hour plane ride, did what he could to help his father. Because the family had little money and poor health insurance, the hospital bills continued to pile up. Dunn got a second job as a bouncer at one of the strip clubs outside Fort Bragg to make some extra money to send home. He was quickly promoted to head of security for his cold calculation and eerie calm during altercations. It didn't hurt that he could do the books better than the strip club owner. The new position allowed Dunn to make more money by getting a portion of the bartender and stripper tips.

One night on the job, a group of rowdy townies decided to make trouble with some drunken soldiers. The soldiers, obviously half in the cups but harmless, were easy targets for the small group of oversized rednecks. Taunted into brawling, the group of three soldiers were no match for the five rednecks. The one black soldier was apparently the target of a torrent of racial slurs hurled by the hulking antagonists.

As Dunn approached the group of brawlers with another bouncer, he noticed the butt of a pistol in one of the attackers' jacket pocket. *Shit. I'm gonna have the ass of whoever let that guy in.*

What started as a shouting match quickly escalated into a melee of flying fists. Just as he reached the guy with the gun, the man pulled the weapon on Dunn. Acting on instinct and training, Dunn closed the final foot, cupped his hands over his head, and pushed the weapon up over his head while simultaneously bending his knees slightly.

The diverted weapon fired and the loud boom echoed in the enclosed space. Patrons and employees screamed as they ran for the doorways. Dunn wrestled the pistol away from the man and clocked him in the temple with the butt. The man fell to the floor unconscious.

Dunn turned to see two of the three bloodied soldiers lying on the ground. The third was being dragged to the door by three of the massive rednecks. The two remaining antagonists turned on Dunn; one with a large buck knife and the other with a pistol matching the one in Dunn's hand.

Still calm but with pistol aimed at the gun-wielding redneck, Dunn made an attempt to diffuse the situation.

"Alright boys, you've had your fun. How about you drop your weapons before anyone really gets hurt?"

Instead of answering Dunn, the largest of the five attackers and, apparently, the leader of the burly band, yelled to his three companions dragging the soldier out. "Bring that nigger over here."

They did as they were told and brought the black soldier, blood pouring from his broken nose, to their leader. As the small group corralled, the remaining club security crew waited anxiously on the sidelines looking to Dunn for direction. *Shit*, thought Dunn. *How am I going to get these hillbillies out of here?*

The tough-talking leader grabbed his captive's shoulder with his hand and positioned the victim between himself and Dunn. Then he put the dazed man in a headlock and pressed the pistol to his left temple.

"What are you gonna do now, tough guy?!"

The rest of the man's cronies laughed evilly as they watched.

Dunn remained calm. "I'll give you one more chance. Put the guy down along with all your weapons and we'll make sure the cops treat you fairly."

The leader laughed. "Boy, you have no idea who you're dealing with. Now, I'm gonna give you thirty seconds to get all the money into a bag and give it to me. If not, your black friend here dies along with a couple more of y'all."

He waved his gun menacingly at the group of security guards. They could tell by his fierce look of determination that the man wasn't lying.

With a clear head, Dunn analyzed the situation. The redneck's last comment told him that the situation had just gone from bad to worse. What at first glance had seemed like a normal barroom brawl, had now escalated into an armed robbery. He knew it would take the local police a few more minutes to get there. Meanwhile, the huge hillbilly was counting down.

Dunn saw bloodlust in the man's eyes and doubted that many would go unscathed even if they gave in to his demands. To make matters worse, two more of the redneck crew had revealed small pistols that had apparently been taped to their lower backs. They all grinned wickedly as if daring someone to make a move.

"Twenty-two... twenty-one... twenty..."

Dunn looked at the club owner, who seemed to barely have the strength to stand. The rest of the employees were quickly gathering cash and wallets to present to the armed robbers. Dunn saw the leader's eyes flicker and a slight grin played across his mouth. The man was actually daring him to act.

"... twelve... eleven... ten... nine..."

Dunn took one last glance around the room and analyzed everything: the location of the armed men, the position of his security crew, the strippers cowering behind the stage curtain, the hostess squatting behind the club owner and the club owner hiding behind the bar.

"... three... two..."

Dunn kept his eye on the man's trigger finger and, just as the man started to say *one*, pulled back the trigger, fully intending to shoot the dazed soldier in the head. Dunn reacted on instinct and double-tapped the huge man in the face. Instead of waiting to see the result, he turned slightly left and double-tapped the other two armed men center-mass. Within a split second, the place was pandemonium again. The black soldier was covered in the now dead leader's blood and gazed up blankly at Dunn. The other two men whom he'd just shot were now writhing on the ground surrounded by security and being stripped of their weapons. The only redneck without a gun quickly dropped his knife in horror and threw up his hands.

The aftermath of the incident confounded and confused Dunn. Instead of being hailed a hero, Dunn was treated like a criminal. With two men dead and another two in the hospital, the local authorities had no choice but to fully investigate the situation.

Despite eyewitness accounts of all the club employees, the authorities could not prove that Dunn was justified in killing the man. He still remembered asking the police about it in the following days.

"Would it have been better if I'd let the guy shoot a man in the head *before* I shot him?"

The system was suddenly against him and the interrogator said as much. The police officer told Dunn that if that had been the case, they wouldn't be having this conversation.

"Look, kid, we don't make up the rules but the law is pretty clear. If this thing goes to court they can paint you into a cold-blooded killer. I already heard that the leader of those redneck boys came from some rich family. They're pretty connected around here and are already raising holy hell to get you the chair.

"But these guys were gonna kill," Dunn argued. "I could see it in their eyes!"

"I hear what you're saying, kid, but I don't make the laws," the detective repeated.

That same police station was where Todd Dunn first met the CEO of SSI. Travis was in Ft. Bragg visiting some contacts and got a whiff of the incident through friends in the Ranger battalion. After making a few inquiries, Travis decided to intervene. He made the visit under the guise of an attorney to gauge Dunn's personality. He walked out of the station knowing he'd just found a diamond in the rough.

Days later, Dunn found himself in a private jet being swept up to some campus in Charlottesville, VA. Apparently this company, SSI, had pulled a few strings and he'd been honorably discharged *and* all charges had been dropped. As he stepped off the plane in Charlottesville, he was met by Travis, now in his casual SSI clothing: outdoor gear and hiking boots.

Travis had apologized for the ruse in the police station and went on to explain what SSI was and find out whether Dunn might be looking for a new job. After coming to the realization that his career in the Army was over, Dunn was quietly overjoyed at the opportunity.

One final piece finalized the deal and Dunn's undying loyalty to SSI and Travis Haden. Not only did SSI welcome

Dunn into their family, Travis also made sure that Dunn's father's hospital bills were paid off completely and that he received follow-up care from the top cancer specialists in the world. Eight years later, the old man was still in remission, and Todd Dunn was enjoying his eighth year as head of security for SSI.

## CAMP SPARTAN, ARRINGTON, TN

"Where do we stand?" Cal asked.

"No blowback from the authorities," Travis said. "No one even knew you were there."

"How about that reporter? Did you get him off my ass?"

Travis sounded exhausted, but he pushed on. "We're still working on that. In fact, it was the Hammer that came up with a rabbit trail for him. It's a good one."

Haines glared at Travis for using her nickname. She was a modest woman despite her fiery spirit and having a nickname like the Hammer didn't help her sense of propriety. Luckily, she and Travis were good friends (and rumored at times to be lovers) and the comments usually rolled off her back.

"Let's just say I threw the guy a bone through an anonymous source and he might be pursuing another more lucrative news story," Haines said.

"I'm not following you, Marge," Cal said.

"It's another operation we're running. Let's just say it won't hurt our cause to have a reporter snooping around. It might actually help us flush a couple of bad guys out."

"So, you're not gonna tell me?"

Haines grinned. "Not yet. You haven't been officially sworn in or given us your blood brother handshake."

Cal shook his head. He always felt one step behind dealing with the Hammer.

Travis held up his hands. "All right, all right. Let's leave Little Cal alone. Todd, any inkling about where this West guy ran off to?"

"Nope. Once the cops lost him, he did a pretty good job digging another hole to hide in. I'm thinking he's probably got safe houses all over town."

"So, you're saying we've got nothing."

"Sorry, boss."

Travis sighed. "OK. So, what's our next move? Any ideas, Cal?"

Cal thought it over for a moment. He didn't really have anything concrete. Maybe thinking out loud would help.

"This last lead was all because of Top Trent. I guess we could send him out again and get him digging. Do we have any other guys that fit into that part of town?"

"We do," Travis said, "but from what you're telling me about this guy, I don't think he'll make the same mistake twice. What do you think, Todd?"

"I agree. I'll bet he made some quick calls to his network and told them to be on the lookout and armor up. I think if we send Willy and some more men up there they might be easy targets."

"What about your link to his cell phone, Neil?" Haines asked.

"Looks like he dumped it. He knew that's how we got a lock on him. That's a dead end now."

Just then the door opened and Dr. Higgins waddled into the room.

Dr. Higgins spoke so formally he almost sounded British.

"Sorry I'm late, everyone. I wanted to make sure the file was ready to scan. Ah, hello there, Calvin."

"Hey, Doc! What file are you talking about?"

Higgins pointed a pudgy finger at Travis. "Ever since your attack, our fearless leader over there has had me building a dossier on Mr. Dante West. Mister Patel, will you pull up the file on this computer?"

"No problem."

Neil walked over to the 52-inch touch screen panel on the office wall and started tapping and scrolling. "Is it in the usual place?"

"It is. My friends, what Neil is about to pull up is not only all the police records we could find, but also my analysis of the man's mental abilities and motivations, along with some video surveillance Neil uncovered."

"Video surveillance?" Cal asked.

Higgins nodded. "Our resident wonder boy Neil was able to hack into some kind of database down in New Orleans. We found a thoroughly entertaining video of Mr. West robbing a local bank."

Travis huffed impatiently. "What are we supposed to get from that?"

"I don't know what you'll *get* from it," Higgins said, "but I was able to determine a lot about our adversary. I won't spoil it for you."

Travis rolled his eyes and looked back to the screen. Neil pulled up the main file. The first image showed a worn file folder with an old photo of West. He looked to be in his teens.

Higgins cleared his throat before diving into the report.

"This, ladies and gentleman, was Mr. West at age fourteen. It was his first formal arrest. From what we could gather, he was implicated in numerous other crimes since the age of ten but had never been caught or arrested. This tells me that Dante West is no fool. Even at a young age, the man was smart and cunning. Apparently, the only reason he was arrested in this instance was because one of his accomplices identified West as being the ring leader. As you'll see on the next page, the boy that snitched was later found brutally beaten in the juvenile detention facility. The informer ended up being paralyzed from the neck down as a result. It was assumed, naturally, that West was the culprit. Once again, the assault charge wouldn't stick to West. We can only assume that the incident taught the assaulted boy a lesson."

"Great story, Doc," Travis said, "but what does this have to do with finding the guy?"

Higgins held up a finger. "Patience, my dear boy. As I was saying, West seems to have a knack for staying under the radar. I looked back through his grade school records and found that in his early years he excelled in academic studies. One report even suggested he had an extremely high IQ, although his school did not have the means to test for it at the time."

Haines sat up a little straighter. "So, what changed?"

"Dante's father was killed when the boy was nine. It looks like his mother turned to drugs and prostitution shortly after. The state soon took Dante out of the home and placed him in a foster facility. It was apparently in that facility that he had his first taste of gang life. The reports from the foster home staff read like a novel. Good kid gone bad. They all talk about how smart he was, a natural leader. He used his authority with the kids to set up his own little gang. They started by stealing food from the kitchen at night and soon escalated to armed robbery. At the age of eleven, he ran away from the facility and never came back."

Higgins took out a handkerchief and wiped his forehead before continuing.

"From the age of twelve on, he was often brought in for

questioning but, believe it or not, they could never charge him with anything. All the police reports detail the fact that he was always respectful, unlike so many of the other young toughs they'd interview. I got a laugh from one entry made by a detective who'd had the opportunity to interrogate West on more than one occasion. This detective actually recommended that the department stop bringing West in for questioning because the young man was, and I quote, 'a squared-away young man with communication skills far beyond the usual perps.' This officer actually submitted the recommendation to the D.A. The whole time they had no idea who they were dealing with."

Cal felt the anger rising in him. "Sounds like you're starting to admire the guy, Doc."

Higgins nodded without an ounce of regret. "Professionally, I do admire him. He is probably a borderline genius with the skill and cunning to elude the authorities. Anyhoo, where was I? West moved up through the ranks in New Orleans and, by his mid-twenties was a top Lieutenant. When Hurricane Katrina hit in 2005, all the local gangs scrambled to claim territory. West's gang came out on top with no small help from West himself. It was never substantiated, but I found two gang task force reports that alluded to West's part in the land grab. Then, all of a sudden, West was gone. Vanished. Through inside sources, the task force pieced together that, as a result of his success in the post-Katrina operation, West was given a promotion. He was tapped to expand the gang's influence to Nashville with the backing of his old gang. Think of it as franchising for gangs. For the last couple years, he's been growing a lucrative trade here in Nashville."

"What do you mean by lucrative trade?" Haines asked.

"It appears that West set up a more structured business than other typical gangs. He essentially uses the gang to protect his assets: drugs, prostitutes, protection, *et cetera*. In another life, Dante West might well have been a very successful businessman."

Cal's temper continued to rise. "Well that's not how he ended up, Doc, so I'd appreciate it if you wouldn't talk about him with such reverence."

Travis kept his voice calm. "He didn't mean anything by it, Cal. You know how Doc is. He looks at all these targets like an author treats a new novel."

Cal took a couple slow breaths. "I'm sorry, Dr. Higgins. I didn't mean any disrespect."

"It's OK, Calvin. I was only saying it's a shame West's talents were... *misaligned*. Sure, his upbringing could have been better, but I'll be the first to admit that we mustn't allow that to cloud our judgment such a man. At some point in his life, Mr. West was presented with a choice as to how he wanted to deal with his unfortunate circumstances. He chose incorrectly. Don't worry, Calvin. We'll do our best to make sure we find Mr. West and bring him to justice." After the visible tension left the room, Higgins continued. "So now the question is 'What will Dante West do next?'"

"Any ideas, Doc?" Cal asked.

"West is a very capable leader and strategist. Looking back on his record, he's never made the same mistake twice. I think he's trying to figure out how to stay out of the hands of the local authorities while at the same time trying to hold his organization together. It's my professional opinion that Dante West is trapped and needs to do something audacious to break out or just sit back and wait. The problem with waiting is that he'll risk losing his associates and possibly lose a lot of his street business. No. I think he'll try to make a move."

"What kind of a move will he make?" Travis asked.

"Something that will solve his problems, get the police off

his track, and get his business back. Maybe an assault on a rival gang? I just can't say for certain. What I can say is that Mr. West is not one to sit back and wait. He is a man of action. He is a man who's built his own destiny. He will not wait to see what happens. I think we need to monitor the police scanners and look into any turf wars or gang violence we might hear about."

Cal sat back in his chair, disappointed. "So, more waiting around."

"Yes, more waiting," Higgins said, looking down at him apologetically. "I suggest you all read his dossier and digest what you can. I am good at what I do, but you may find something I didn't. It's all I can think to do for now."

Cal nodded and moved to shake Dr. Higgins' hand. "Thanks for your help, Doc. I appreciate your insight."

"Not at all, Calvin. I'll continue my analysis and let you all know if I find anything new."

With that, Higgins waved farewell and left the room. Cal and the others had no doubt that SSI's resident mind specialist would spend many sleepless nights analyzing and reanalyzing West's file. Once on the trail, Dr. Higgins was a true bloodhound. He wouldn't stop until his quarry was found.

Cal turned back to the others. "Any other thoughts?"

"I'll do some digging, too," Todd offered. "Maybe my contacts within the police department and FBI can help. Couldn't hurt."

Haines stood up. "I'll run some checks through my court contacts. See if we can't run down some of his associates and squeeze some intel out of them."

"I'll reach out to some of my contacts, too," Travis said. "Let's all remember to be discreet about this. The last thing we need is that reporter catching wind of this."

The small group dispersed and Travis followed Cal out.

"Hey, Cal. Got a minute?"

Cal nodded and led the way to his father's office two doors down. Even though it'd been years since his parents' deaths, the office was still in the same state that Cal Sr. had left it in 2001. The office was cleaned daily by a crusty old Marine who'd served with Cal Sr. in the early 1970's. Although now technically retired, the old Marine came in every weekday to reverently dust and vacuum "The Colonel's Office."

# TILLY

Cal remembered first meeting the man years ago. Leonard Tilly had left the Marine Corps after serving in Vietnam. He'd been a machine gunner in then-Capt. Stokes's company. Back in those days, the military wasn't given the same place of honor as in the post-9/11 days. The proud Marine returned home to find protesters spitting at him and calling him names. Worst of all, upon returning to his family he found that his twin sister (the two had been inseparable from birth) now dressed in hippy garb and spewing the same propaganda he'd heard debarking the airplane ride home. Even after repeated attempts to make peace with his sister, he finally gave up.

Unable to settle in or even find a job, he learned to cope through drugs and alcohol. Instead of dealing with the pain and emotional grief, he internalized his pain and went into a quick downward spiral. Within a year, the poor man was living on the streets begging for money so he could buy a hit or swig. Leonard Tilly spent the rest of the 1970's and 1980's bouncing from shelter to shelter and bottle to bottle.

In the mid-90's Tilly had somehow wandered to the

Nashville area. By that time, the Stokes family was back in Nashville and Cal Sr. was reestablishing his roots and expanding his business. One weekend as father and son were volunteering at a local shelter handing out food, Cal Sr. spied Tilly in the line. Now hunched, his body ravaged and aged by years of abuse, the prematurely old man shuffled forward in his oversized winter coat. On his left arm he'd sewn on a tattered Marine Corps emblem. Cal Sr. liked to chat with the people they volunteered to help and used the patch as his introduction.

"Nice patch you got there. Were you in the Corps?"

The crusty marine looked back at him suspiciously. "Yeah. So what?"

"I was in the Marine Corps too."

Tilly paused and tried to concentrate his gaze on his fellow Marine. Without thinking he blurted, "I was in Vietnam."

"Me too. Those were different times, weren't they?"

Finally, the man's smile cracked. Cal Sr. could see his filthy teeth, but also noticed the sudden gleam of remembrance in the man's eyes.

"They sure were. Different times."

Over subsequent visits, Cal Sr. made it a point to keep track of Tilly and check up on him. Cal remembered asking his father why.

"Because he will always be a Marine," his father said. "That makes us family. If he wants help, I'll give it to him."

The two Marines had quickly made the miraculous discovery that the homeless Tilly had once served under Cal Sr.'s command. Not surprisingly, Cal's father put great effort into helping "his Marine." Over time, Tilly agreed to enter a rehabilitation program paid for by the charitable arm of Stokes Security International.

After getting cleaned up and reunited with his family, he

was offered a position in the newly built SSI complex just south of Nashville. After years of substance abuse, Tilly's mental capacity was now diminished. He was, however, extremely grateful for the chance to help maintain the grounds for SSI. Over the next few years, he became one of the company's most loyal employees. Refusing, even after numerous offers from Cal's father, to call Cal Sr. anything but Colonel, Tilly was once again home among his fellow warriors. He ate in the chow hall and shopped in the small PX. This was indeed his home.

Upon Cal Sr.'s death, Leonard Tilly wept openly as he demanded from Travis that he be allowed to maintain the Colonel's office as a sort of shrine. Travis had relented.

After officially retiring, Tilly was given a comfortable living space in one of the campus' small homes.

# CAMP SPARTAN, ARRINGTON, TN

Needless to say, the office was spotless as Cal and Travis walked in. Cal often came to the office to sit and stare at the countless photographs all around the office. There were pictures of the family and of his time in the Corps. Anyone visiting the office could see that Cal Sr. had somehow found a way to merge his two families into one through the birth of SSI. It was his legacy and would serve as a home for warriors for years to come.

Cal still remembered what the place had looked like during construction. His father always enjoyed nature and had his office designed so that it appeared to be part of the outdoors. The office itself actually jutted outside the main structure of the building and close to the surrounding woods. It afforded the office a 180-degree view of the surrounding area. You could sit in the office early in the morning and watch the deer and turkey grazing below.

Cal walked around the large desk and sat in the cushy swivel chair. Travis took the seat in front of the desk. He always deferred to his younger cousin when visiting the office together.

"So, what do you think, cuz?"

"I'm thinking that I'm about tired of waiting," Cal said. "We got all geared up for that trip north only to have it fizzle out on us. It's just a little frustrating."

Cal answered while mindlessly opening drawers and peering in just as he had done as a teenager. He'd always been curious about what his father kept close at hand.

"I understand how you feel, but you've got to realize that this is the real world. Middle America. We can't just go around guns blazing shooting up the bad guys."

"I'm not an idiot, Trav. I'm just disappointed."

"I know, man. But listen, if nothing else, this is good experience for you for later on. If you decide to be an active part of SSI, you need to learn about the rules. You might as well learn them now."

"Alright, I'm game. Hit me with the high points."

Travis drew a deep breath. "OK. Like I told you before, these types of operations started a few years ago. We saw the need and we attacked it. Also, we were approached by certain entities that needed work done on the sly. We've always been really careful with whom we work with. We are not vigilantes for hire. We are also not a tool for corrupt politicians or criminals. The work we do here in the states beneath the law is strictly regulated and kept under the radar for obvious reasons."

"So, who approves these missions?"

"Right now, me. Back in the day, it was your dad. There are only five of us within SSI that are actually involved in decision making for these ops. Todd Dunn and the Hammer are two of the five. Dr. Higgins is obviously in the loop. Last, but not least, is Neil. Between the five of us, we make the call whether to use company assets or not."

"What about the teams you send out to do the dirty work?"

"They are never, and I repeat, *never* in contact with any individual or group that initiates the mission. That's my job. I think I mentioned before that some of the people that tip us off are highly placed government officials. It is absolutely necessary that they maintain plausible deniability."

"Trav, I hate to say this, but you're starting to sound like you're running some kind of secret society. Do I have to learn the secret handshake too?"

Travis didn't laugh. "I'll give you the benefit of the doubt because of who you are, but this shit is serious. Now do you want to hear this or not?"

Cal threw up his hands in surrender. "Sorry. Go ahead, Grand Master."

A small grin spread on Travis's face. He was a man that rarely displayed anger, but Cal's comment had obviously hit a nerve. It was hard not to give his cousin a little ribbing every once in a while. Tough habit to break.

"Like I was saying, our sources are really funny about their involvement. We've obviously vetted everyone but we've always gotta be careful. That's why each mission is always reviewed by the five of us before we decide to make a move. Every angle has to be explored and the good and bad always have to be weighed. As a result, we don't green-light every mission. Sometimes we decide not to act and our sources understand that. We can't be everything for everyone."

"So how do you decide which mission you do green-light?" Cal asked.

"There's no real formula. It really comes down to a couple of things. One: do we think we can get away with it without being exposed? Two: does the result of a successful mission, and its positive effect on this country, outweigh the possibility of failure AND exposure Three: does the mission live up to the standards of Corps Justice? If any one of those things can't be answered definitively, we don't move forward. Sometimes we'll go back to our sources and tell them thanks but no thanks and give them a recommendation on who should handle the problem."

"Can you give me an example of a mission you refused?"

Travis thought for a moment. "Three years ago, one of our sources came to us with an interesting dilemma. Apparently, one of the big Mexican cartels was hiring American engineers to dig these elaborate tunnels under the border. The problem was that law enforcement didn't have the manpower to track down the leads and exploit the intel, so they came to us. We looked at the intel and asked what they wanted done. Basically, they wanted us to shut down the operation. We ended up not taking on the mission, although we did provide them with some of Neil's toys because we didn't see the direct result it was having on American security. Now don't get me wrong, I'm not all about the cartels bringing their drugs into our country, but we just didn't feel like it was a worthwhile operation for the amount of effort we'd be putting in."

"So what if the cartels were running terrorists through those tunnels and not just drugs?"

"That would've been another story. We hate terrorists around here; especially the ones that try to sneak into the country. But you need to understand that we get A LOT of requests and we're only one company. As much as it sucks sometimes, we can't say yes to everyone."

"I think I've got a better picture now." Cal looked his cousin in the eye. "So, tell me how you think I'd fit into the equation."

"Honestly, I just don't have the time to run it anymore. It's not that we run a lot of ops, it's just dealing with our sources and going through the thought process. As CEO, it's probably best that I don't run it anyway. Too much visibility. I'll still be involved but I think you've got the brains and experience to run it."

"Trav, I'm a Marine Staff Sergeant. You're talking about running a covert arm of this company. I'm not sure I'm really qualified to do that."

"You'll have help. Dunn, Haines, Patel and Higgins to start. And don't forget that I'm not going anywhere either. Don't worry, we're not just gonna throw you to the wolves on day one. We'll ease you into it."

Cal was skeptical. "That sounds like what my company gunny said before I took over as platoon sergeant."

"This ain't the Marine Corps, cuz. SSI is a well-oiled machine. Besides, not to pump up your ego too much, but you've got a lot of your dad's talents. The guys around here already respect you and think you're part of the team. Anyone gives you grief, I'll deal with them. Plus, is there anyone else in this world that we could trust more to run our covert ops? I think not."

Cal mulled it over. Is this really what he wanted to do? He'd always respected his father's company and the men in it, but running what was essentially a division within a multi-billion-dollar corporation at his age was almost too much to fathom.

The sun had already set as he thought about what else to ask his cousin. Cal obviously didn't need the money. He'd considered going back to school, maybe heading back to UVA to finally finish his degree. He couldn't go back in the Marine Corps. It was still entrenched in two wars and he'd already gotten funny looks from those who knew about the Navy Cross. He loved the Corps but that chapter was finished. He couldn't go back.

Besides, this might give him the opportunity to actually do some good without being bogged down by rules of engagement or meddling by higher headquarters. He could think of a lot worse options out there

"So, you're saying that at some point I'd have final say in any operation we take on?" Cal asked.

"Yep."

"Do we have a name for this quote, unquote division?"

"Not really. I call our inner circle the Fantastic Five but no one thinks that's very funny. I guess if you want to name it, you can. I wouldn't recommend going out and getting business cards though."

Cal nodded. The idea was starting to grow on him.

# N.O.N. SAFE HOUSE, NASHVILLE, TN

Dante looked around at his underlings. All were armed and ready. They'd taken the remainder of the afternoon to inventory their gear and finalize plans.

"Any questions?"

The gathered men shook their heads. They knew the plan. It wasn't a complicated one.

"Alright, let's get going."

West led the way to the back of the house and out the door. Their vehicles were waiting and fully gassed. They'd all been serviced earlier in the week per West's instructions. He was not about to let a low oil light or a faulty transmission screw up this night's action.

The assault crew piled into their respective vehicles and cautiously pulled out of the driveway. After the episode with the police earlier, everyone was on edge.

The caravan made its way out of town and onto the interstate. It would be a short twenty-minute ride to their destination. West was almost giddy with anticipation. He calmed his nerves as he always did: by imagining a mental picture of a dead Cal Stokes.

———

CAL AND TRAVIS talked until the sun had fully set. There were still a lot of details to be ironed out once the former Marine had made his final decision, but Travis was confident that Cal would come around.

"So, like I said, Cal, sleep on it and we'll talk about it again over the next couple of days. Right now, your focus needs to be tracking down West."

"OK. Give me a day and I'll give you a decision one way or another. How about we—"

Cal felt his cell phone vibrate in his pocket. He pulled it out and checked the caller ID.

"I'd better take this, it's Frank. You wanna wait, or see you tomorrow?"

"I'll catch you in the morning," Travis said. "Give Frank my best."

Travis got up out of his chair and turned to leave. Cal picked up the call.

"Hey, Frank."

There was a pause on the other end.

"Frank can't come to the phone right now, if you'd like to leave a message please wait until the sound of the gun shot."

Cal's blood froze. He knew the voice well. He had heard it over and over in his brain since waking up in the hospital. Dr. Higgins had it right: Dante West had made his play.

Travis turned to wave goodbye and apparently noticed the pale expression on his cousin's face. He quickly walked back into the room and shut the door.

"What happened?" he whispered.

Cal grabbed a piece of paper and pen from the desk and scribbled: *It's West. He's got J's parents.*

Travis nodded and grabbed his own cell phone. He speed-dialed the emergency number for the SSI alert system.

Within minutes, the entire internal management team would be assembled in the war room and the quick reaction force would be mobilized.

Cal turned his attention back to the call. "What do you want?"

"I guess I don't need to formally introduce myself. By the tone of your voice, it sounds like you already figured that one out."

"What have you done with Jess's parents?"

"Oh, nothing yet. Just a couple of bruises. Old man wanted to fight back so we had to smack him around a little."

"I swear, if you touch them—"

"Now let's not start making promises you can't keep, hero boy. How about we get down to business before I have to cut this call off."

"What do you want?" Cal repeated.

"I want *you*, Mr. Stokes. So, here's the deal. I want you to come meet me and some of my friends. If you act nice, we'll exchange you for the husband and wife. If you call the cops or do something stupid, they die."

"How do I know you'll keep your word?"

"You don't, but what other choice do you have? From what I've read online, you're the hero type. I seriously doubt you'll let these old-timers die."

What other choice did Cal have? At the moment, he couldn't think of another option than to agree. "OK. Where do I go?"

West relayed the address and Cal wrote it down.

"What time do you want me there?" Cal asked. His hand was shaking.

"Let's say one AM. That way we'll have the place all to ourselves. Come alone."

"I'll be there."

"See you then, hero."

The phone went dead and Cal stood and stared out the window. The moon was almost full and he could clearly make out the surrounding trees. The forest seemed eerily calm, as if anticipating the impending confrontation.

Travis gave Cal a few seconds to gather himself before he spoke. "What did he say?"

"He says he'll let them go if I give myself up."

Without a direct reply, all Travis could do was nod. He knew it was better not to give an opinion until the team had gathered. "I've already alerted the headquarters staff. They should be gathering in the war room right now. Let's go see if we can figure this out."

Cal managed to grab his notes and followed his cousin out the door. Doubts swirled in his mind as he tried to focus on some kind of solution.

His mind reeled at the twist. *How did I not see this coming?*

## WILLIAMSON COUNTY, TN

Dante replaced Frank's cell phone on the kitchen table and turned to his prisoners. They were sitting on the floor flanked by two of West's men.

"Looks like your boy is gonna pay us a little visit. You both behave and you might get to go home."

Frank glared at the gang leader through hate-filled eyes. "You leave Cal out of this, you murderer!"

"Now, now, grandpa. That's no way to treat your host. Don't make me put you to sleep again. Better yet, how would you like me to give your lady a little time with a couple of my boys here?"

"You touch her and I'll kill you!"

Dante responded with a kick to the man's stomach. Frank doubled over and retched on the floor.

"Now, see what you've made me do? Like I told you when we took you out of your house, you keep your mouths shut and you just might make it out of this. If not, I can't make any promises."

He threw up his hands to accentuate his point, as if the choice were completely out of his control.

Frank looked up again and put his arm around his quietly sobbing wife.

Dante rubbed his hands together. "Now we've only got a few short hours to wait. My boys will take you back to the master bedroom and tie you up so you can get some sleep. I'll come get you when the time comes."

West waved a casual dismissal and the two guards pulled the prisoners to their feet and took them to the back of the house.

Dante turned back to the window and repeated the phone conversation over in his head. He'd always had the ability to find the calm within the storm. His analytical brain outshone any of his competitors. Many had underestimated his talents. His was a gifted mind that catapulted him up through the ranks. That, coupled with his ruthless tactics, would see him rise once again.

*My redemption nears.*

# CAMP SPARTAN, ARRINGTON, TN

The SSI inner circle gathered in the secure conference room down the hall from where Cal and Travis had just been. Each member walked in quietly and waited for the information. This was not their first emergency session.

Travis took a seat at the head of the table and the rest arrayed themselves close by. Cal stayed standing as he continued to pace the length of the room.

"Cal," Travis said gently. "Why don't you give everyone a quick rundown of the conversation you had with West?"

Cal did in a tone that suggested his mind was already searching for possibilities.

"OK," Travis said, looking around the room. "We've got about four hours until Cal needs to be there. The good news is that as smart as West is, he has no clue that Cal's got SSI assets behind him. Anyone have any questions or comments?"

Todd spoke first. "I think we need a few teams to infiltrate into the area right now. We can take them in low with the two helos we have on site and drop them in about a mile away. Hell, there's so much farmland out there the launch will be easy. After landing the teams, the helos can take up station and give us some video using their infrared cameras. We should be able to get a damn good idea of who's with him and the layout of the place."

Travis nodded. "OK, get it done."

Dunn grabbed his phone, slipped to the corner, and made the call in clipped, whispered commands.

"What else?" Travis asked.

Neil was next. "I'll make sure all the teams have multiple drones at their disposal. They'll each be rigged with non-lethal darts. Might help take out some of West's friends."

Travis nodded and pointed to Dunn. "Go talk to Todd and make sure those guys don't leave without getting as many of your toys as possible. I mean it, Neil. Anything they need."

"Got it."

Neil got out of his seat and headed over to chat with Dunn.

"Who's next?"

"I know I'm asking the obvious," Higgins said, "but have any of you cowboys thought about how young Calvin is going to get out alive?"

"I'm not worried about that, Doc."

"I understand. You will, however, be going in unarmed into the lion's den, as they say."

"Doctor Higgins is right, Cal," Travis said. "It won't do anyone any good if West gets his hands on you."

Cal's voice was steel. "I don't care about me right now. I need to get them out of there. If that means I go in alone, then I'll go in alone."

"I know you're upset, cuz, but you need to take a step back on this one. If you don't, you'll be playing right into his hand."

Neil stepped back into his spot and snapped his fingers. "Dammit!"

"What?" Travis asked.

"I can't believe I didn't think of this before. I've got a couple of things that might be able to help Cal out."

"You want to elaborate, Mr. Wizard?"

Neil was full of energy. "Let me run down to the Bat Cave and grab a few more toys. It'll be easier to show you than to explain. I'll meet you guys outside."

He ran out of the room with an excited, almost childlike, grin on his face.

Travis shook his head. "I don't know sometimes with him. OK, so who else has a brilliant idea? Marge, you got anything?"

Haines thought for a second before she answered. "Clearly, you guys have the operational stuff taken care of. I'm just trying to think of the aftermath. Anyone give a thought to what we do with the any bad guys you might capture or, worst case, kill?"

Cal answered immediately. "We take out anyone we need to. I'll deal with the consequences later."

Haines shook her head. "I know you're upset, but that's not how we run around here, Cal. We *have* to think about the next step. For instance, if we do take prisoners, what do you do with them? Especially if they've seen your face. We have to make absolutely sure that SSI is not linked to the rescue."

Cal blew out a breath. "Sorry, you're right. So how do you guys usually do it?"

Travis rubbed his chin. "If it's something overt like this we usually wear masks or face paint at least. It really depends on the situation. It'll be hard for you to do that. So, the question again is, what do we do with West and his henchmen?"

"I know I'm the most amped up about this, but what if, worst case, we just kill them all? I'm not a murderer or anything but these guys asked for it, right?"

"True," Travis said. "But then you've still have to think about the fallout. Disposing the bodies is no big deal. Jess's parents are another problem. We can't have them blabbing about this team of guys dressed in black coming to save the day."

"I thought Frank and Dad were good friends. Doesn't he know some of what we do?"

"Sure, but not at this level. I guess we just have to be careful about how much we expose them to."

"I agree," Haines said. "The less they know, the better. If it ever comes to sitting on the witness stand, I want them to have plausible deniability. They need to be able to say they didn't see anything and don't know anything."

Todd looked up from his phone and called across the room. "Hey, Trav. We've got the two helos warming up and we've got six two-man teams getting ready. I've got 'em suiting up in black with suppressed weapons and non-lethals. Along with night vision and Neil's toys, they should be good. Anything else?"

"Nope. That sounds perfect. Tell them we'll meet them at the helos in ten minutes."

Dunn nodded and continued to relay his orders through his cell.

"All right," Travis continued. "Let's all go grab whatever gear we'll need and meet back up outside."

Everyone left the room knowing it was going to be a long night.

# CAMP SPARTAN, ARRINGTON, TN

The assault teams and supporting staff met ten minutes later at the PT field that doubled as an expedient landing zone. Andy and Brian were both suited up in identical black utilities. MSgt Willy Trent stood nearby talking with Dr. Higgins and Marjorie Haines. Todd Dunn was giving the assembled troops their final orders while Travis listened and chimed in periodically.

Neil wandered around the pairs of assault men handing out his goodies. Each pair nodded as they were handed their gift bags. They all knew Neil well and always liked getting to try out his array of new gadgets. These were all highly skilled operators with extensive real-world experience. Warriors, one and all.

Cal walked around the group not really knowing where to fit in. He was a key part of the operation, but he still felt disconnected. Everyone else knew their part and none had hesitated to come to his aid. It was in that moment, as he observed the silent preparation of each man, that he finally felt at home. A feeling of peace wrapped itself like a blanket around his body and mind. The clarity of battle suddenly enveloped him. He knew what he had to do.

He stepped up to the men that would put themselves in harm's way and asked for everyone's attention.

"I wanted to say a couple words before we step off. First, although I think I know the answer, any man that feels uncomfortable with the upcoming mission and the possible repercussions can leave right now."

He looked around at the gathered men and none stirred. Until someone chuckled. It was Travis. Then the laughs spread to the assault teams.

Cal knit his eyebrows together. "Didn't anyone ever tell you not to volunteer for anything?"

The snickers changed to outright guffaws as a smile spread across Cal's face. One of the men in the back row shouted. "We don't have a choice, Staff Sergeant. You sign our paychecks!"

Cal laughed. It was good to be with his family again. Another man in the front row joined in the ribbing, pointing at Travis.

"Shit, I didn't volunteer. The recruiter screwed me."

Cal held his hand up for silence. "As long as we understand each other, I just wanted to say thanks. I feel like I'm back with my Marines."

Another voice rang out. "Semper Fi, Staff Sergeant!"

A fourth man joined the chorus. "Ooh-rah, Staff Sergeant!"

Followed by a din of barks and backslapping, the men lined up to shake Cal's hand. He somehow held in his emotions of gratitude and he looked each man in the eye as they all quickly shook his hand and boarded their respective helicopters.

As the last man boarded, the pilots of each helo looked to Cal, saluted and lifted off.

Travis walked up behind Cal and put a hand on his cousin's shoulder. "Well I guess I know what your answer is."

"Yeah. I'm in."

———

IT WOULD BE a short twenty-minute car ride out to the location where West held his captives. It gave them a chance to finalize their strategy.

They had devised a plan that would both keep things simple and maximize their chances of success. Cal would drive MSgt Trent's truck to the rendezvous point while the others – Travis, Dunn, Brian, Neil, Andy and MSgt Trent – would board one of the returning helos and fly to a nearby loitering area. It would allow them to monitor the situation and provide almost immediate support if needed.

Neil explained his new gadget to Cal and the others as he helped him put it on. "Just remember, since this is a prototype you'll only get one shot with it. It doesn't have the ability to recharge yet."

"Got it," Cal said. "One helluva way to field-test it."

"Yeah. You'll owe me a full debriefing when you get back."

Patel paused, and both men knew why. The tech guru had suddenly realized there was a high probability that Cal would not return.

"No problem," said Cal. "I can't wait to use it." He'd seen the change in Neil's demeanor and wanted to diffuse the sudden tension. Patel relaxed and slapped on his quirky smile once again. "You're a genius, brother.

Trent stepped up to them. "I'd really like to see the look on West's face when you use it."

Cal nodded. "To rehash really quickly: once I get eyes on Frank and Janet, I give you guys the signal and you send the teams in. I'll take care of West."

"Yeah. Just remember to keep your head down when our boys come crashing in," Trent warned. "I told Dunn not to use flash bangs so you should be good there. With any luck, those Baby Birds will take out a few bad guys. Hey, Neil, you got the helo cams up yet?"

Neil had resumed his position in front of the numerous computer screens. "Almost there. They just called in to say the insertions were successful."

"Can you patch that through your speakers?" Cal asked.

"Just a sec." Neil played out a few keystrokes. "Got it."

The small group looked over Neil's shoulder to see the live stream from the two helicopters. They'd positioned themselves at a distance and altitude that wouldn't allow their locations to be heard from the farm held by West and his crew.

"Spartan six, this is Spartan Mobile Two."

Travis answered. "Go ahead, Mobile Two."

"Roger, how does my video feed look, over?"

"Clear and pretty, Mobile Two."

"Roger, zooming in for a closer look."

The group stood transfixed as the pilot zoomed in on the main house. It appeared to be a one-story ranch. The infrared camera easily picked up the heat signatures in and around the house.

"Six, I've got what looks like twelve bodies on location. You getting this, Six?"

"Roger, Mobile Two," Travis said. "Can you really get it there with the zoom and pan around the house, over?"

The pilot did as instructed and panned from room to room. There were six people in the house itself. Four were in what looked to be a back bedroom or master suite.

"Zoom in some more on that back room, Mobile Two."

"Roger."

The screen enlarged and the team could see the white

outlines of two people sitting on the ground and another two pacing around the room.

"That's gotta be them."

Travis nodded. "Mobile Two, can you give us a better look at the perimeter?"

"Roger." The video slowly zoomed out and panned around the property. "Six, I've got what looks like four teams of two patrolling the perimeter, over."

Silence reigned as the team continued to follow the moving video. Each man was analyzing the battlefield in a different light. They could already make out the patrol patterns.

"Are we patching this to the assault teams?" Travis asked.

Neil nodded. "I gave them some tablets that have the video streaming live. Each two-man team has one."

"Good. I want to make sure we're all seeing the same things."

They continued to watch the live feed knowing that the landscape they now observed would soon be underfoot.

———

THE FOURTH PATROL had just checked in. Nothing but a bunch of deer and turkey. His boys weren't used to farm landscape but none had complained. They knew better than to gripe now. West walked to the master bedroom and addressed the captive couple.

"You have about another hour until your hero gets here. Don't go thinking you're gonna try anything. Both of my boys here have orders to shoot you if you run. Don't worry though. I told 'em only to shoot you in the legs. It'll hurt like hell, but it's better than being dead."

The bound pair said nothing for fear of more beatings. They'd already silently agreed to wait until Cal showed up.

They believed in Cal's abilities and, more importantly, Frank secretly hoped SSI would be involved.

———

"You ready, Cal?" Trent asked.

"Yeah. Thanks again for loaning me your truck."

Trent grinned. "No problem. I know if anything happens to it, you'll buy me something better."

"You bet."

Travis came over to join them. He had the look of brotherly worry already etched on his face. "Are you ready?"

"Jeez. How many dads do I have around here? I'm fine, Trav."

Travis shrugged, but he didn't look sorry. "Had to ask."

"I know."

"Anything else you need?"

"How about you have a nice glass of The Famous Grouse waiting for me when we get done?"

"You got it. But really, Cal, are you sure you're ready for this? You did just get shot like two weeks ago."

"I'm still a little sore and weak, but I'm not planning on doing any of the heavy lifting. I'll let the assault teams take on the bad guys."

"Good. Like we talked about, keep your head down and our boys will take care of the rest."

Travis patted him on the back. Cal nodded and jumped in the truck. He had to adjust the front seat to accommodate his smaller frame. Starting the engine, he looked back as his friends gathered next to the truck.

"Alright, boys, I'll see you on the other side."

He closed the door and didn't look back. Pressing on the gas, he wondered if this would be the last time he'd see them.

DANTE PLAYED the scenario out in his head. He knew that the Stokes kid would probably try something. Hell, he'd try some little trick too if he was in the same boat.

It didn't matter though. The plan he had concocted couldn't even be foiled by an FBI raid. Revenge was fast approaching.

# WILLIAMSON COUNTY, TN

C al pulled into the dirt driveway that led to the appointed rendezvous point. He knew the assault teams were simultaneously tracking their targets and getting ready. Taking a deep breath, he drove the oversized truck up the lane.

Around a bend, he caught the winking beam of a flashlight. He figured it was probably two of the guards sitting by the interior fence. Sure enough, as he pulled up he saw two thugs armed with rifles flagging him down.

He slowed and approached the gate.

The guard's voice was hard. "Get out of the truck."

"OK." Cal complied and slowly opened the truck door. He came out with his hands raised.

"You have anything on you?" the guard asked.

"Just my cell phone."

The guard shouldered his weapon and expertly frisked Cal. He took out the cell phone and gave the other guard a thumbs-up. Then he turned back to Cal.

"Get in the truck. We'll be in the back with our guns pointed at your head so don't try anything stupid."

"I wouldn't think of it."

The three men climbed into the truck and one guard directed Cal to drive up to the house. Cal did as instructed and they made it to the modest structure without further interference.

The other guy in the cab ordered Cal out of the truck. For the second time that night, Cal carefully stepped out of the cab. He looked up to the porch and saw another thug standing in front of the door. He motioned for Cal to come closer. Once again, Cal was subjected to a thorough frisking. These guys weren't messing around.

The first guard handed Cal's cell phone to the house guard and walked back to the truck.

A third guard pointed at the house. "Go in through the door right there. Dante's waitin' for you."

Cal nodded and headed to the door trailed by the third guard. He opened it and stepped inside. The guard motioned to the right. Cal walked towards what he knew was the kitchen. As he moved, he imagined the assault teams quietly moving into their final positions, drawing beads on West's patrols.

He walked into the kitchen and tensed as he saw the familiar face of Dante West.

"Welcome to my humble abode."

"Where are Jess's parents?"

"Right down to business, huh." He yelled to whomever was in the other room. "OK, bring them out."

Cal heard footsteps and waited anxiously for his one-time future in-laws to appear. They shuffled slowly into the room. Jess's mother looked disheveled and scared. Frank's appearance made Cal's blood boil.

"Are you guys OK?" he asked, his voice trembling with rage.

"We're fine, son," Frank said.

"I thought you said they wouldn't be touched."

Dante shrugged casually. "It's not my fault the old guy wanted to put up a fight."

"You're going to regret touching them."

"I don't think you're in a position to do much threatening, white boy. So, anyone tracking you with that cell phone?"

"I told you I was coming alone. Now let them go."

Dante spoke to the guard with Cal's cell. "Take the battery out of the phone and give them to me."

The man did as ordered and gave them to Dante. West looked at it briefly then put it in his right pant pocket.

West pointed to his two prisoners and spoke to his men.

"Take these two out back and get rid of them. I'll take care of the hero."

Cal screamed. "You *motherfucker*!"

Cal lunged at Dante. The man side-stepped and watched Cal drop to the floor.

"It's time for you to take a nap, white boy."

West pulled out his pistol and slammed Cal in the back of the head. The last thing Cal remembered before blacking out was a foggy image of a screaming couple being dragged out of the house.

―――――

"OH, SHIT." Neil said.

Travis leaned over his shoulder. "What?"

"Cal and West just disappeared."

"What do you mean they disappeared?!"

"One second they were there, clear as day, on the infrared video screen, then there was a scuffle and the two disappeared."

"Could they be in a basement?"

"It's possible, but we'd still have even a weak signal if they were in a typical basement."

"Wait," Andy said. "What if it's not a typical basement?"

Travis looked up at him. "What do you mean?"

"Neil, what does it look like on the screen when someone walks into a secured bunker?"

"They disappear."

Brian chimed in. "But this is a normal house."

"That's what it looks like from the outside," Andy said. "Neil, can you pull up the ownership records for the property again?"

"I've got it right here."

"OK. It says here that the property was quitclaimed over to some entity called Williamson Enterprises, LLC," Andy said.

"Yeah. I already looked that one up. It looks like a typical shell entity used to hold real estate."

"What if this LLC is controlled by West?"

Neil quirked an eyebrow. "You really think he's that sophisticated?"

"You heard what Dr. Higgins said. This guy's been under-estimated his whole life. I think he owns this property and has built something under the property."

Travis held up a hand. "Is that even possible?"

"I wouldn't put anything past this guy, Trav. You better tell—"

Neil interrupted Andy. "Hey, guys, it looks like some of the guards are dragging Jess's parents outside."

Travis spoke into his microphone. "All teams, this is Six. Mission is a go. I repeat, mission is a go."

————

SILENTLY IN THE DARK NIGHT, each of the teams launched

their quiet drones. Every man knew how critical it would be to hit their targets with their one and only non-lethal shot.

In staggered intervals, each team took out their targets with swift precision using the drone's dart capability, save one.

The pair dragging the prisoners outside got halfway to the backyard before one of the men was immobilized. The second gang member bent down to pick up one of his stumbling prisoners just as the dart meant for his neck sailed harmlessly high and into the side of the house.

Standing back up, he looked to his left and noticed his partner unconscious on the ground.

"What the fu—"

Two muffled rounds in the face silenced the man forever. The assault team moved in quickly to secure Jess's parents.

Each pair called in to Travis to report their success.

Travis spoke to his companions. "All of West's men are secure. One dead. They've got the parents and are moving to the evac LZ."

"What about Cal?" Brian asked.

Travis shook his head. "There's no sign of him. The house is empty."

Cal awoke to find himself strapped to a two-wheeled dolly by a set of orange vehicle tie-downs. He was being carted down what looked like a narrow tunnel with intermittent lighting. It was cold, musty, and damp as he tried to get his bearings. Suddenly the dolly stopped and West stepped around to face Cal.

"You awake?"

"Where are we?"

"Where nobody will find us."

"Underground?"

"Not as dumb as you look, white boy."

"Where are you taking me?"

"I guess I can tell you now. Once my boys take care of your girl's parents, they're gonna join us down here. Then the fun starts. Before that happens, you'll get a little tour of my facility here."

Without further explanation, Dante moved back behind Cal and started pulling the dolly again.

Cal's eyes were wide as they kept moving farther into the

hillside. They soon passed rooms full of marijuana plants and high-powered halogen lighting. It looked like they had one impressive growing operation down there. It was no wonder West could keep operating even on the run. Cal decided he'd try some questions.

"You want to tell me how you built all this?"

Dante's voice was filled with pride. "The economy's in the shitter. For the right price, we had some really good contractors down here building for a while. We even had a couple of consultants from the Army Corps of Engineers. I got the idea from something I read about a redneck here in Tennessee who built something similar for his weed-growing but got caught when someone noticed how much electricity he was using. We solved that problem. We're entirely off the grid. No one knows this place exists."

"What about the guys that built it? You can't keep their mouths shut."

"We were choosey about who we picked and where they came from. Shipped them in from a couple of states and kept them on property until they were done."

"Are you telling me they're still working?"

Dante chuckled. "Sort of. They're fertilizing the local vegetation now."

So that was it. He promised to pay a king's ransom and then he killed them. Higgins was right. This guy was smart and ruthless. Cal decided to keep trying to build rapport.

"How did you guys get around the power problem?"

"That was the easiest part. My boy in the White House decided to start giving out tax credits for new energy sources like solar and geo-thermal. We've got a huge geo-thermal footprint all around the underground tunnels. On top of that, we've got dedicated generators powered by everything from gas to solar. Not bad for a kid from the hood."

"Is this your only facility?"

"Now why do you think I'd tell you that?"

"I figure you're probably going to kill me, so what's the harm?"

"Fair enough. We've got a total of five of these babies scattered around Williamson County. Three are operational. We get to make our goods right under one of the richest counties in the nation. We're starting out with marijuana then we'll probably get into the meth business. That's what you white boys like, right?"

Cal was impressed by the size of the underground facility. The sheer magnitude of dirt moved illustrated the power of West's burgeoning empire.

The problem: How the hell was he going to get out?

———

THE ASSAULT TEAMS gathered on the front porch listening to Travis give orders. The incapacitated gang members had been quickly interrogated. Not one knew anything about the secret tunnel they'd just uncovered. Worse still, the one man who probably could've helped had been killed. He'd apparently been Dante's number two.

To complicate matters even more, the door they'd found behind the rotating shelving in the walk-in pantry was built like a bank vault. From what they could tell after a cursory examination, the steel door was some five inches thick. One of the assault teams was already trying to cut through the door. West had covered his tracks well.

Travis spoke up. "So, here's the plan: the assault teams will stay here and keep trying to cut through this damn door. Willy, you stay with them and lead the way in. The rest of us will jump in the two helos and take a look around. There's an exit somewhere, we've just gotta find it."

"What about Cal?" asked Andy.

"The best we can do is find him fast. There's no telling what West has planned for him."

———

CAL REMAINED silent as they neared their final destination. West wheeled his guest into what looked like a butcher shop mixed with a crude third world hospital clinic. Cal could feel the cold air and smell the residual stench of some kind of meat. The dolly came to a stop.

"Where are we?" Cal asked.

"This is my own private interrogation chamber. Over there, you can see some of my tools. Picked up the trade from this ancient voodoo man in New Orleans. Taught me some good tricks to get men talking. Really useful when you think one of your boys is a snitch."

Cal stayed quiet as he gazed around the room. He noticed an old rusted bedspring in the corner anchored to the floor and ceiling. Next to it was a pair of car batteries with cables. Next to the cables was a bench with an assortment of knives and tools. Everything looked well-cared-for and well-used.

"You want to tell me why you're going to torture me?" Cal asked.

"It's called revenge, brother."

"It's not enough that you killed my fiancé?"

"You killed my crew *and* you crippled my business. I owe you change."

Cal wasn't getting anywhere with his questions. He needed to try something else. When in doubt, try the frontal assault.

"For a guy as smart as you, I'd think a pussy move like attacking a harmless couple was a dumb move."

Dante froze. "What the fuck are you talking about?"

"Shit, Dante, I heard you were a pretty smart guy back in

the day. I guess all that dope you've been slinging gets harder and harder to say no to."

"You don't know a thing about me, motherfucker."

"I know about your dad and how he died. I know about how your mom gave you up when you were a kid."

Dante stopped what he was doing. His eyes went wide then flashed with anger. He also registered a touch of unease in response to Cal's comment. How could this white boy know that? It was never in the papers. He'd made sure his past had been buried a long time ago. It was amazing what he could snag with a couple quick break-ins.

"You made that up."

"Oh really? Then ask me how I know that you've got a really high IQ and that up until the age of ten you were doing well in school."

"Who have you been talking to?"

Cal laughed. "You dumb shit. Obviously there are things about me that you don't know."

"You better watch your mouth. Looks like you forgot who's in charge."

"Really? I'd say in the next couple of minutes my boys are gonna be coming through that door over there."

"Who, the cops?"

"No, asshole. Tell you what, why don't we leave it as a surprise?"

West stared hard at his prisoner. "You a gang leader now?"

"Wanna try me?"

"You know why I don't believe you?" Dante said.

"Why?"

"Because I designed this place myself. Oh, I forgot. You were passed out when we passed through not one but three doors built like bank vaults. It'll take days to cut through that shit."

Cal tried to gauge whether the gangster was bluffing or

not. Either way, one of them would be right soon. Cal could only hope that his friends would find him quickly.

## MAIN HOUSE, N.O.N. COMPOUND, WILLIAMSON COUNTY, TN

"Six, this is Big Dog." It was MSgt Trent.

"Go ahead, Big Dog," Travis said.

"We've got a little issue here. We got enough of a hole cut to see through the other side with our fiber optics. Looks like there's another door on the other side some ten feet down the passageway."

"You're kidding me."

"You know I wouldn't do that, Six."

"Alright, keep working and we'll do the same. Let me know if you have any other ideas. Six, out."

Travis looked to his companions and gave them the news. West was surprising them at every turn. What looked like a straightforward mission now felt like a complete clusterfuck.

"Anyone else have any bright ideas?"

Andy rubbed at the back of his neck. "I think we need to start by getting half of your teams roaming the countryside. Who knows, they may get lucky and find the tunnel exit."

"What about the toy I gave Cal. You think he'll use it?" Neil asked.

"I'd think he would've used it by now," Travis said.

Andy looked worried. "OK. Then let's keep sweeping the countryside and see what we find."

The companions fell silent and continued to look out the windows with their night vision goggles. Each kept toggling back and forth between normal night vision and heat register. Nothing yet.

―――――

WEST HAD GONE BACK to preparing things in the room. Cal was curious about why his captor hadn't called his goons yet. Maybe they worked off cell phones and the signal couldn't penetrate the underground lair.

Cal had one more ace up his sleeve: the weapon Neil had given him. The problem was its deployment would be tricky. He somehow had to get West to use the cell phone he'd confiscated. That would take some coaxing.

*Think, Cal, think.*

An idea popped into his head like a lightning strike. His plan wouldn't be easy and he'd have to feel some pain first. No matter. It was his only option. Cal gritted his teeth and steeled himself for the upcoming torture. He knew from talking with former POWs that everyone broke eventually. The body and mind could only take so much.

He would have to use that to his advantage.

"Are you gonna get started or do I have to torture myself, pussy?"

Dante looked back in surprise. "You still think you're gettin' outta this, don't you, white boy? Think again. Oh, and you may wanna watch your mouth and enjoy the last few minutes you've got."

"Whatever. Any second now my guys will be busting in that door over there."

"Not likely. The back exit to this place is impossible to

find. Plus, this won't take long. I'll be outta here and leaving your body to rot after I'm done with you."

"So, are you going to tell me why you want to torture me? Not for nothin', but revenge kinda sounds like a bullshit answer."

Dante grinned. "At first it was all about revenge. You see, I can't let the asshole that put me on the radar and killed my boys get away with it. The second reason came to me a minute ago while you were running your mouth. I'm curious about these so-called secrets you say you have. It might be a good investment of my time to do a little digging."

*Bingo!*

Dante moved back to the dolly and pressed his pistol to Cal's temple. "Now I'm going to unstrap you and take you over to the bedspring. You try anything, I'll shoot you. You got me?"

"Yeah, I got you."

He released Cal slowly, not once allowing the gun to slip. He ushered his prisoner over to the bedspring that was now connected to the two car batteries. West methodically strapped Cal to the metal frame with zip ties on his ankles and wrists. Cal was spread-eagle, glaring at West and prepared for pain.

"I'll start with a low setting," Dante said. "I just want you to get a little taste."

West switched the machine on and Cal heard the buzz of electricity. Next, Dante grabbed the power knob and turned it to the first setting.

Cal's body seized and his eyes shut involuntarily.

This wasn't going to be fun.

———

TRAVIS WAS AGITATED. "All the teams just checked in.

Nothing from the guys scouring the farm. Neil, are you finding anything in those property records?"

"Nothing. Obviously no plans were ever submitted to the local commissions for the building. Looks like he really did it on the sly."

"What about the police records? Any complaints for noise or blasting?"

"Already checked that and no. Besides, this property is just shy of a thousand acres. They could get away with a lot without ever being seen or heard."

"What about the topography?" Brian asked.

Travis turned to him. "What do you mean?"

"I know there's a lot of land in the hundred-year flood plain around here. I would assume that if West wanted a long-term facility he would've factored that in. Maybe we can find out which way the tunnel leads by taking away certain portions of the topography."

"Good idea. Neil, pull up all the topo maps with elevation and flood plain data. It's the only lead we've got right now."

————

WEST HAD JUST SHOCKED Cal for the third time. He had yet to ask a single question. It was obvious he was just enjoying seeing the pain register on the former Marine's face.

Cal, although in extreme pain during each shock, was starting to finalize his plan. It was a strange talent he'd uncovered while on the battlefield in Afghanistan. He'd found that in times of extreme pain and duress, his mind became hyperfocused instead of losing its edge and dissolving into fog. It was what had allowed him to keep going even after being wounded multiple times.

Within this clarity, he remembered hearing stories from former POWs from the Vietnam War and World War II.

They'd survived by divulging mere snippets of the truth. They'd survived by effectively weaving lies within the truth. Cal was about to try the same tactic.

Cal was panting. "Are you gonna ask me any questions or just get your rocks off watching me shake?"

"Man, you must really have a death wish. You ready to die already?"

"No. I'm just ready to be done with your bullshit."

"Still hoping your buddies are coming to save your ass, huh?"

"That's right. And when they do I'm gonna strap you to this fucking thing and let you go a couple rounds."

"Hate to tell you this, boy, but that ain't gonna happen. How about we just get down to the questions. This time we're gonna play a new game. If I think you're not telling the truth, I turn on the machine again. If I *really* think you're bullshitting me, I'm only gonna beat on you a little bit."

Dante picked up a steel baseball bat from the corner and demonstrated practice swings. His grin returned.

"What, no knives yet?"

"Oh, those will come soon enough. So, let's get to the questions."

———

MSgt Trent pulled at the heavy steel door with all his strength. They'd finally cut around the locking mechanism. Sweat beaded on his brow as the door finally separated from the last bit of steel holding it to the lock.

The door swooshed open and the assault team quickly jumped into the space, guns at the ready, panning for targets.

The leader called out. "All clear!"

Trent eyed their next obstacle. "Does it look like the same kind of door as the first one?"

"It does, Top. You want us to start cutting again?"

"Do it."

The team leader nodded to his demolitions expert and the man moved quickly to the next door his cutting tools already in hand.

Trent spoke into his mic. "Six, this is Big Dog."

Travis answered immediately. "Go ahead, Big Dog."

"First door breached. Moving to breach door number two, over."

"Roger. Let me know as soon as you have an idea of what's on the other side."

"Roger, out."

Trent was praying there wouldn't be a third door.

———

WEST HAD BEGUN the interrogation with some basic questions: date of birth, home address, sexual preference, etc. It was obvious that West was building some kind of rudimentary baseline to see if he was lying; sort of a gangster version of a lie detector test.

"Time for some real questions," Dante said. "How did you find out about me?"

"My company."

"What do you mean your company?"

"I own a company."

"What kind of a company?"

"A consulting company."

"This is your one and only warning. Stop trying to drag this out. You answer me or I'll make you answer it. You got me?"

"I thought I was doing damn well, asshole."

Without warning, West picked up the baseball bat and took a quick swing square into Cal's gut. Cal tried to dodge and somehow absorb the blow. His head sagged as the wind was knocked out of him.

"You've got thirty seconds to catch your breath and then you start answering."

Cal could feel his recent gunshot wounds throbbing and threatening to bleed again. He had to stay focused and buy more time. The only problem was how much more could he take.

*Hurry up, Trav.*

———

ANDY CROSSED his arms over his chest. "The best I can see is that the tunnel has to run this way under this ridge line. Any other way, they risk going into or at least skirting the flood plain."

"I'm still not totally sold on the idea," Travis said.

"I think West would've thought about this. The guy went through Hurricane Katrina and probably the flood of 2010 here in Nashville. He doesn't strike me as a guy that would take any chances."

"OK. So where does the tunnel dump out?"

"I say we start right over here by the Harpeth River. We might—"

"I just had another idea!" Neil interrupted.

"What?" Travis asked.

"Let's assume that West is using this place as some kind of drug manufacturing center. Even if he's able to mask the heat of his power source, he'll still need to have some kind of exhaust."

"Explain that."

"It's like a car engine. All that heat has to go somewhere. The intake and exhaust help keep the engine cooled. If West is using heat lamps, for example, that hot air has to go somewhere. It would be crazy expensive to have a self-contained system like they have in a nuclear sub. I'm betting they had to build vents to get the hot air out."

"Then shouldn't we see them with our heat vision?" Travis asked.

Neil shook his head. "Not necessarily. The scopes we use are calibrated to see obvious variances, like the difference between a person's body temperature and the ambient air temperature."

Andy cut through their conversation. "But then how do we see people at night when we use the same scopes in the desert?"

"There's still a difference between your body temp and the air temperature," Neil said. "It's just that the air's warmer."

"So how do we find these vents?" asked Andy.

"Let me see if I can patch into the helo's infrared system and recalibrate it for much smaller variances."

"All right, but do it fast," Travis said. "The longer we take, the less I like Cal's chances."

———

WEST WAS GETTING MORE and more excited as the interrogation went on. He'd already found out about SSI and Cal's stake as owner. Who would've thought he'd catch the heir to a billion-dollar company? The options started to whirl in Dante's head.

Maybe he could ransom Cal.

Maybe he could exchange his prisoner for money and weapons.

The possibilities were endless.

"You're in luck, rich boy. I'm thinking that you might just make it out alive today."

Cal looked up through puffy eyes and spit more blood onto the floor. His insides were on fire and his tongue felt like a puffed-up marshmallow. Every time he got shocked, he swore he'd bitten off another piece of his tongue.

Dante smiled down at him. "What's wrong? No more smartass comments?"

Cal's voice was thick when he answered. "What do you want me to say?"

"How about you give me the number to someone I need to call at your company? Maybe I can talk to someone sane there."

"I don't know the number. It's on my cell phone."

Dante glanced down at his pant pocket as if he'd forgotten the missing cell phone. He pulled the cell phone and battery out. "How do I know they won't track me as soon as I put this battery in?"

"Aren't you the one that told me cell phones don't work down here?"

"True."

"So how the hell would they track it?"

"OK. So, what's the phone number?"

"Call my cousin Travis. It's under T. Or wait, you can read, can't you?"

West shook his head and looked back down at the phone. He replaced the battery and turned the phone on. Cal watched expressionless, waiting for the perfect moment to reveal his surprise. He wondered if he'd even be able to reach the trigger Neil attached to his right molar with his tongue.

Neil had instructed him to tap the molar three times and the miniature flash bang he'd installed within Cal's cell phone would detonate. The problem now was getting his swollen tongue to react at the right moment.

Cal moved his numb tongue around in his mouth and spat

another gob of blood and phlegm onto the floor. He looked back to Dante.

"This thing is asking for a password. What is it?"

Cal gave Dante the access code and instructed him on how to retrieve the correct phone number.

"You may want to try making the call from the phone. It's got enhanced signal strength and could work," Cal offered.

"I thought you said it wouldn't work down here."

"It's worth a shot. Might get you through faster, unless you have a better idea."

Dante glared at him for a moment and then shrugged. "What the hell."

Dante speed dialed Travis's number and held the phone up to his ear. Just as it reached his ear, Cal carefully tapped his molar three times.

The cell phone exploded.

West collapsed to the floor, his hearing in his left ear thoroughly wiped out. He lay unconscious as Cal tried to find a way out of his restraints. Neil had been very clear on the last point. West would only be incapacitated for a maximum of three minutes. Cal had to hurry.

The team on the helicopter waited anxiously as Neil patched into the onboard system and clicked away.

"I've almost got it. There."

Everyone looked expectantly at the video monitor to see the change. Neil had been right. What had looked before like only a few spectrums now looked like a rainbow where every color bled into the next.

Travis' voice rose. "You want tell me how the hell this helps us?"

"Patience, Travis."

"I'm about out of patience, Neil. My cousin, your *friend*, is down there right now having that fucking gangster do who-knows-what to him. He might already be dead."

Andy placed a hand on Travis' shoulder. "We don't know that, Trav. Neil's doing his best. So, show us how this works, Neil."

Neil pointed to the monitor. "Now this is all just theory, but I'm thinking that if we zoom in close enough we might be able to see the vents."

Travis began to calm down. "What are we looking for?"

"It should almost look like a little fire," Neil said. "You know how you look at a flame say coming out of a pipe? I'm thinking if I got the calibration right, we'll be able to see that."

The group spent the next minute staring at the screen as Neil zoomed and panned over the terrain. Brian almost jumped out of his seat pointing.

"What's that right there?"

Neil leaned closer. "Let me zoom in. That looks like a vent! Now let me follow it up this way..."

"There's another one!" Andy shouted.

"Good job, Neil," Travis said. "Now keep following those vents and let's see if we can find that damned rabbit hole."

———

IN UNDER A MINUTE, Cal had somehow managed to scrape the zip tie on his left wrist almost all the way through on the rusted bed spring. He gave one last tug and the tie popped off of his bloodied wrist.

He glanced back down at the still unconscious West. His internal clock told him he probably had less than a minute to get out. He was in no condition to find out if his body could handle a hand-to-hand fight right now.

———

THE HELICOPTER CREW tracked the vents to a location just over a mile from the main house. There they found some kind of tiny structure that appeared to be a sewer drain. Travis decided to start the search on the ground there.

After hearing from MSgt Trent that there was a third

steel door behind the second, Travis ordered Trent to leave two men to guard the house and bring the rest via helicopter to the possible tunnel exit.

Travis spoke to the pilot, pointing to an open spot below. "Put her down right over there in that field. We'll hump the rest of the way."

"Where do you want me?" Neil asked.

"Stay on the helo and give us updates from the air. Doc, I want you ready with whatever medical gear you have."

"Roger," Brian answered.

"Andy, how do you feel about going in first?" Travis asked.

"I'm game."

"OK. The rest of us will provide support."

The pilot spoke up. "Ten seconds to LZ."

"Roger," Travis said, surveying his team. "Let's go get our boy."

———

CAL HAD ALMOST REMOVED his last restraint when Dante started stirring. He looked up in confusion and shook his head trying to clear the cobwebs. Attempting to focus, he got up to his hands and knees just as Cal snapped the last zip tie off of his left ankle.

With speed that surprised Cal, Dante got to his feet and reached in his pocket. Staggering on unsteady legs, Cal snatched the baseball bat from the ground, swung it back-handed, and connected with West's firing hand just as he extracted a pistol from his coat.

The weapon fired and clattered to the floor as Dante clutched his hand.

He looked up at Cal. "You're gonna pay for that, boy."

Dante stepped backed and grabbed a wicked looking filet

knife from the bench. Cal was trying his best to stay on his feet but his head was reeling. His body had taken a real beating. He had to focus. His life depended on his ability to stay on his feet.

———

## N.O.N. UNDERGROUND FACILITY BACK EXIT, WILLIAMSON COUNTY, TN

Andy led the reinforced team up to the iron sewer grate that was mounted into the side of the hill. The crisscrossed iron bars were big enough to fit an arm through, but no way near big enough to fit a person. The stench was foul. He could see water draining out through his night vision goggles. It smelled like it came from a local cow farm. Sweeping the area, he looked for some kind of entrance. Where the hell was the exit? Looking back to his left he stopped.

"Did you hear that?"

Trent nodded. "Sounded like a muffled gunshot."

"Yeah. Came from inside the grate. You think you can move it?"

"Let me take a look."

Trent shouldered his weapon as the rest of the team provided cover. The huge man felt around the edge of the grate for some kind of release or handhold. Nothing. Next, he reached inside the opening and started methodically feeling along the inner edge. Halfway around he stopped.

"I think I've got a handle here but it's locked."

"Where are the hinges?" Andy asked.

"On the left side."

"You think we can blast through it with a little demo?"

"Won't that give us away?"

"I think it's a little late for that. Besides, I didn't like the sound of that gunshot a second ago."

Trent nodded his agreement. "OK. I'll go get the breach kit from our guys."

Andy nodded and looked back to the grate. *I hope it's not too late.*

―――――

THE TWO WOUNDED men circled each other trying to find an opening. They each eyed the pistol on the ground. The weapon would easily turn the tide.

West took a quick swipe at Cal. Cal dodged easily and shifted left as West moved closer to his lost gun.

"I can't wait to carve you up, white boy."

"You're the one with half an ear. Looks like I'm winning."

Dante put his hand up and touched the remains of his tattered ear. Although wounded, he was far from being out of the fight. The loss of hearing in his left ear wasn't going to stop him. West looked at his opponent with pure hatred. Only one man would be leaving alive.

West was convinced he would be that man.

―――――

THE TEAM STEPPED BACK and took cover as the signal was given that the breaching explosive was set. Andy counted down with his fingers and the demolition man pressed the button on the remote device.

At the same moment, the loud blast echoed through the trees.

Andy looked around the tree and saw that the grate was now resting on its hinges. They were in.

―――――

CAL AND DANTE looked toward the open hallway at the sound of the muffled explosion. Fear crossed Dante's face as he quickly calculated his options. He still had an extra escape route in case the back sewer was found.

Cal grinned. "I told you my boys were coming."

"They're not here yet," Dante said, but he sounded shaken.

As he spit out his last word, he lunged for the discarded pistol. A second later, Cal was also diving for the weapon. He was too late. As he descended to the floor, Cal could see Dante wrapping his hand around the pistol and turning his way. The world slowed as Cal stared down the barrel of his executioner.

———

THE TEAM RUSHED into the tunnel scanning and clearing as they went. They kept as quiet as they could, but the running water made it almost impossible. Andy pushed hard as he moved down the tunnel. Fifty feet down he found a door. Luckily, this one wasn't made of steel.

———

CAL LURCHED to the right as the Dante pulled the trigger. Miraculously, the bullet somehow only grazed Cal's head as he descended the final distance to the ground. The side of his scalp burned from the bullet's passing. He ignored the pain and tried to knock the weapon aside.

Dante brought the pistol back around towards Cal. This time he wouldn't miss.

———

MSGT TRENT BARRELED through the wooden door like a freight train. Andy came in right behind with his weapon leveled. He could see light ahead and heard the sound of another gunshot.

―――――

INSTEAD OF SHYING AWAY from the gun, Cal embraced it... literally. He grabbed Dante's pistol hand and tried to angle the barrel up as he pulled the weapon closer to his chest.

A crash sounded from the hallway and Cal could see Dante struggling to keep his focus inside the room. For Dante West, the next few moments would seal his fate regardless of whether he lived or died. His only hope now was to exact his revenge before that happened.

―――――

ANDY RAN down the tunnel trailed by the rest of the assault team. His heart pounded as he readied himself for the scene he was about to encounter. Would Cal be dead? Rounding the corner his heart leapt as he saw his friend struggling on the ground with West. *Still alive.*

―――――

DANTE'S EYES widened as he glanced at the hallway to see men in black streaming into the room. The two men grappled on the floor, a fight to the death. The pistol remained lodged smack in the middle of the two. A hairs breadth either way and one man would be dead.

Cal and Dante lay locked in a deadly embrace, eyes blazing and desperate. West's finger still gripped the pistol trigger. Cal struggled to point the gun back at West. Cal saw his opponent pull the trigger twice and felt the loud double report of the gun.

———

THE ASSAULT TEAM WATCHED HELPLESSLY, not wanting to take a shot for fear of hitting Cal. His friends each felt the two gunshots deep in their guts. They all screamed at once as Cal slumped to the floor.

# EPILOGUE

## CAMP SPARTAN, ARRINGTON, TN

The funeral was a private affair. All of Cal's and Jess's friends attended.

They'd decided to dedicate a new cemetery on Camp Spartan itself. With some heavy legal work by Marge Haines, they were able to get the approval of the state and local authorities. The deceased was family after all.

The grave site was situated on a lonely hill overlooking the rifle range. It afforded a magnificent view of the surrounding countryside. According to Travis, it was where Cal had taken Jess for their first picnic on the campus grounds.

Cal Stokes stood flanked by his closest friends, looking down at the casket holding his beloved Jessica. Although still gripped with grief, his head and heart had turned the page. She would never be forgotten, but Cal could live free of guilt. The death of Dante West had closed that chapter for Cal. He could now move on as Jess wanted.

The service was short but beautiful. Jess's pastor presided

over the affair with grace and dignity. It never ceased to amaze Cal, as he stood surrounded by some of the fiercest warriors he'd ever met, that such men often held the most compassion and emotion. It was what allowed them to do what they did to the best of their abilities and protect fellow Americans that often criticized their methods and spat in their face. These were men of duty and honor.

Among the tear-stricken brave, he was finally home.

———

CAL SAID his final farewells to Jess's parents and split off to rejoin his friends. Travis cut him off before he got there.

"How you doing, Cal?"

"Still a little bruised up, but I'm OK."

"It's only been a week. You'll have plenty of time to heal now."

Cal's voice sounded absent. "Yeah."

"Hey, I know this might not be the best timing, but I've got some people I'd like you to meet."

"Here?"

"Actually, down at the Lodge."

Cal raised an eyebrow. "How about a hint?"

"It's a little hard to explain. Why don't you tell the guys we'll meet them at the bar in about an hour. The Sergeant Major's bringing out the good stuff."

———

TRAVIS LED the way down the second-floor corridor of the Lodge. Cal could see two burly men in suits standing outside one of the large suite doors. *What the hell?* He decided to keep his mouth shut and follow Travis's lead. *I guess I'll find out soon enough.*

Travis nodded to the two guards as one mumbled into his lapel mic. Following his cousin into the suite, he noticed the backs of nine men as they entered. Each man was dressed in casual attire but even their clothing couldn't dampen their air of dignity and power. They came in varying shapes and sizes but all seemed familiar to Cal and apparently with each other.

The tallest guest turned as did the other eight at hearing the sound of the door closing. Cal almost tripped as he recognized each and every man, not from personal acquaintance, but because in the suite stood nine of the most powerful American political leaders of the last two decades, including three former U.S. Presidents.

"Gentlemen, allow me to introduce my cousin, Cal Stokes. Cal, say hello to the Council of Patriots."

———

I hope you enjoyed this story.
**If you did, please take a moment to write a review ON AMAZON.** Even the short ones help!

**>> GET A FREE COPY OF THE CORPS JUSTICE PREQUEL SHORT STORY, *GOD-SPEED*, JUST FOR SUBSCRIBING AT HTTP://CG-COOPER.COM <<**

# ALSO BY C. G. COOPER

**The Corps Justice Series In Order:**

*Back To War*

*Council Of Patriots*

*Prime Asset*

*Presidential Shift*

*National Burden*

*Lethal Misconduct*

*Moral Imperative*

*Disavowed*

*Chain Of Command*

*Papal Justice*

*The Zimmer Doctrine*

*Sabotage*

*Liberty Down*

*Sins Of The Father*

**Corps Justice Short Stories:**

*Chosen*

*God-Speed*

*Running*

**The Daniel Briggs Novels:**

*Adrift*

*Fallen*

*Broken*

*Tested*

## The Tom Greer Novels

*A Life Worth Taking*

## The Spy In Residence Novels

*What Lies Hidden*

## The Alex Knight Novels

*Breakout*

## The Stars & Spies Series:

*Backdrop*

## The Patriot Protocol Series:

*The Patriot Protocol*

## The Chronicles of Benjamin Dragon:

*Benjamin Dragon – Awakening*

*Benjamin Dragon – Legacy*

*Benjamin Dragon - Genesis*

## Stand Alone Novels

*To Live*

# ABOUT THE AUTHOR

C. G. Cooper is the *USA TODAY* and AMAZON
BESTSELLING author of the CORPS JUSTICE novels
(including spinoffs), The Chronicles of Benjamin Dragon and
the Patriot Protocol series.

Cooper grew up in a Navy family and traveled from one
Naval base to another as he fed his love of books and a
fledgling desire to write.

Upon graduating from the University of Virginia with a
degree in Foreign Affairs, Cooper was commissioned in the

United States Marine Corps and went on to serve six years as an infantry officer. C. G. Cooper's final Marine duty station was in Nashville, Tennessee, where he fell in love with the laid-back lifestyle of Music City.

His first published novel, BACK TO WAR, came out of a need to link back to his time in the Marine Corps. That novel, written as a side project, spawned many follow-on novels, several exciting spinoffs, and catapulted Cooper's career.

Cooper lives just south of Nashville with his wife, three children, and their German shorthaired pointer, Liberty, who's become a popular character in the Corps Justice novels.

When he's not writing or hosting his podcast, Books In 30, Cooper spends time with his family, does his best to improve his golf handicap, and loves to shed light on the ongoing fight of everyday heroes.

Cooper loves hearing from readers and responds to every email personally.
*To connect with C. G. Cooper visit*
www.cg-cooper.com

Made in the USA
Lexington, KY
24 October 2018